NEW BLOOD

DON'T MISS THESE OTHER THRILLING NOVELS IN THE WORLDS OF

Last Light
Troy Denning

Saint's Testimony
Frank O'Connor

Hunters in the Dark
Peter David

Broken Circle
John Shirley

THE KILO-FIVE TRILOGY
Karen Traviss

Glasslands
The Thursday War
Mortal Dictata

THE FORERUNNER SAGA
Greg Bear

Cryptum
Primordium
Silentium

Evolutions: Essential Tales of the Halo Universe
(anthology)

The Cole Protocol
Tobias S. Buckell

Contact Harvest
Joseph Staten

Ghosts of Onyx
Eric Nylund

First Strike
Eric Nylund

The Flood
William C. Dietz

The Fall of Reach
Eric Nylund

NEW BLOOD

MATT FORBECK

BASED ON THE BESTSELLING VIDEO GAME FOR XBOX

GALLERY BOOKS
New York | London | Toronto | Sydney | New Delhi

G

Gallery Books
An Imprint of Simon & Schuster, Inc.
1230 Avenue of the Americas
New York, NY 10020

First Gallery Books trade paperback edition March 2016

GALLERY BOOKS and colophon are registered trademarks of Simon & Schuster, Inc.

For information about special discounts for bulk purchases, please contact Simon & Schuster Special Sales at 1-866-506-1949 or business@simonandschuster.com.

The Simon & Schuster Speakers Bureau can bring authors to your live event. For more information or to book an event, contact the Simon & Schuster Speakers Bureau at 1-866-248-3049 or visit our website at www.simonspeakers.com.

Interior design by Leydiana Rodríguez
Cover art by Isaac Hannaford

Manufactured in the United States of America

10 9 8 7 6 5 4 3 2 1

Library of Congress Cataloging-in-Publication Data is available.

ISBN 978-1-5011-2808-0
ISBN 978-1-4767-9670-3 (ebook)

ARCHIVIST'S NOTE

After the incident on Talitsa in 2555, each surviving Spartan was thoroughly debriefed in light of the salient issues raised concerning conflicting emotions and loyalties among the subjects of the SPARTAN-IV program. Edward Buck's unusual candor proved illuminating at this crucial juncture in the institution's history, in the years after the end of the Human-Covenant Conflict (also referred to as the Covenant War) and in the early development of the Spartan branch. His story is presented here in its entirety for placement in the historical record.

ONE

Report of Spartan Edward Buck
Office of Naval Intelligence Eyes Only

I never wanted to be a Spartan. They didn't even exist when I was growing up on Draco III, unless you count the citizens of the Greek city of Sparta back on Earth, I suppose, but that's one hell of a stretch.

The super-soldiers from the SPARTAN-II program, like the Master Chief? Back when I was a marine, they always struck me as glory-hungry bullet-catchers. And I wasn't just your average grunt slinging slugs for the United Nations Space Command. For the better part of my career, I was one of the top soldiers in the human part of the galaxy, the ones the regular marines look up to.

I was an ODST.

That's an Orbital Drop Shock Trooper. We're the ones who get packed into our high-tech coffins and then shot out of perfectly good spacecraft. From there, we zip through skies burning with enough ordnance to turn a regular ship to slag, then slam down behind enemy lines and start clearing the LZ for the next wave of marines lining up behind us.

We had a damn hard job, and we did it better than anyone.

The old-school Spartans? The best thing they did for the rest of us on the field of battle was draw enemy fire.

That's no small benefit, mind you, and I got nothing against the Master Chief himself. I've met him. Fought alongside him. He's a good Joe. You know, for a genetically engineered superhuman who was kidnapped at six years old to be shaped into a killing machine.

He never morphed into a monster and tried to bite my head off. Not once.

That's a far sight better than I can say about those Covenant bastards we put down together. And don't even get me started on the Flood. (So far, I've managed to avoid coming into contact with those nasty critters though. Not coincidentally, the docs tell me that's the best way to prevent *any* kind of infection.)

But times change. Spartans change. Hell, even I changed.

The Covenant War ended. We won. With the help of the Arbiter and his rebellious Elite pals, we kicked the rest of their bifurcated asses off Earth, and then we cleared out every human system we could find.

Go, humanity! Am I right?

I loved that. The moment we knew we'd won? That was a sensation I'll never forget. Against all odds—and countless thousands of Covenant troops—humanity had survived.

One thing overwhelmed me even more than that feeling of triumph: a sense of relief.

But that stunning instant of accomplishment faded faster than a perfect sunset on shore leave. We might have shattered the Covenant as a group, but some of the most hostile surviving bugs picked up the pieces and did their level best to glue the damn thing back together into an even uglier version of its old self.

Now, I didn't mind that so much, but without the threat of the original, properly organized Covenant looming over our heads, some of the *human* rebel forces who had joined the UNSC in our fight against the aliens didn't cool their barrels for more than a couple days before they spun their sights on the rest of humanity again. Never mind that without the UNSC's efforts, they'd have been mosquitoes on the Covenant's windshield. They weren't the kind to get choked up over such favors.

So while the war might have been over, the battles went on, just over different issues.

I kinda miss the old days. At least then, you knew who to shoot and who might be drawing a bead on you. But as Commander Musa likes to say, you don't always get to fight your favorite foes.

He also likes to say that, as Spartans, we no longer have formal ranks like they do in the rest of the military, which we're supposed to take as meaning we're all equals within the Spartan branch of the UNSC. Course, some of us are far more equal than others, and he's the main point of evidence for that. So I don't take his words as gospel.

Don't think I'm knocking inequalities, as long as they're justified. I used to like being a gunnery sergeant in charge of my own squad.

Anyhow, that's how me and what was left of my ODST fireteam—code-named Alpha-Nine—found ourselves on Talitsa in August of 2555, almost three years after the end of the war, hunting for a Covenant Engineer named Vergil and his human handler, Sadie Endesha. Note that I said *his* and not *its*—we've come a long way with the Covenant.

We'd been sent to that damn dustball by Veronica—excuse me, Office of Naval Intelligence Captain Dare—who thought we might have some kind of rapport with the alien. I suppose I saw her point. After all, Alpha-Nine had been the team that'd hauled his floating carcass out of New Mombasa, back on Earth in

October of 2552, at the worst point of the Covenant War. If he had the capacity to recognize us, maybe he'd still be grateful for our help, assuming ONI hadn't abused him too much in the interim.

I wasn't about to put any money down on Vergil knowing me from any other leatherneck. Me, I couldn't tell him apart from another Huragok without a visual assist from my armor's heads-up display, even though he was the only one I'd spent any real time with.

At least he didn't insist I call him Quick to Adjust, which, to be fair, was his real designation. Vergil was just the name of a program inside the AI that had run New Mombasa's infrastructure, which got damaged when the Covenant invaded the city. While Quick to Adjust was trying to fix it, he assimilated Vergil into his own programming, and the name somehow came along with it. That's how we first came to know him, and it kinda stuck.

Mostly because "Vergil" rolls off the tongue better, I think.

"You have a better chance with him than anyone else," Veronica had said to me. "Plus, you're one of the best soldiers I know."

"Just *one* of the best?"

"I know a lot of soldiers these days." She gave me a kiss on the cheek and that little wry smile she has when she knows the argument's already won. "And there are a lot more Spartans out there now."

I suppose that's fair if you count the Spartan-IVs, the new ones like me. We're not exactly like those artificial gods from the earlier generations. More like demigods. And I'll be damned if that usually isn't good enough.

"And who's the handler?" I asked Veronica. "Her name sounds familiar."

"You have some history with her, although you've never met her."

"How's that?"

"Sadie is the daughter of Dr. Daniel Endesha, the man who programmed the Superintendent AI that ran New Mombasa. As a single father, he couldn't watch over his daughter as much as he wished, so he coded the Superintendent to be her caretaker instead. He called the program that did that Vergil."

"Ah." Now it started to make sense.

"That's why I gave the Huragok that name. It's also why ONI decided to pair Sadie up with him later."

"Because the program that was set to watch over her is now a part of him." I scratched my head. "Does that mean the Huragok looks after her like a father?"

Veronica shrugged. "It means he has an attachment to her we haven't seen him form with any other humans. In fact, that's how the United Rebel Front got their hands on him. They kidnapped Sadie, and he went along, quiet and willing."

"What the hell were they doing on Talitsa in the first place?"

I started rolling my eyes before she could finish saying, "That's classified." She then held up a finger to cut me off. "But I can tell you that the UNSC has been using the ongoing conflict against the Front there as a proving grounds for the MJOLNIR armor project."

"And Vergil might have been giving them a hand. Tentacle. Whatever."

"I didn't say that, but does it matter?"

Not really. It was a shitty job either way, but then that's why they called *us* in.

Romeo started whining about it as soon as we were on the ground on Talitsa. Our ONI ride had dropped the three of us off in a rocky valley several klicks away from our target, which meant we had to hoof it the rest of the way, and he didn't care for the effort one bit.

"It's bullshit, Gunny." Romeo still used that nickname for me when we were out of earshot of the other Spartans, as did Mickey. Force of habit, I suppose. "What's the deal with making us walk?"

"Afraid you'll get a blister on your dainty little feet?" Mickey said as he scanned our six with his designated marksman rifle. He didn't care for the idea of a hike any more than Romeo did, but he wasn't about to pass up an easy chance to razz his old pal some.

Romeo kept his eyes fixed on the mountain rising against the horizon before us. "Back in the day, they'd stuff us in our coffins and boom us right down on the bugs' heads. Now they're afraid we can't manage a proper insertion?"

"We come cracking down through the sky like that, and the rebels holding Vergil will pop him—her, it, whatever—like a meaty balloon." I started to leg it toward the rust-colored mountains, following the suggested route on my HUD, which wound about more than I liked. The others fell in behind me like birds in formation. "Since our mission is to save him from the rebels, we'd prefer to avoid that. We don't have a lot of Engineers on our side to spare—which is why we can't let the Front have even just one."

"But it's okay if they kill the girl?" said Mickey.

"Sadie's not a girl. She's only three years younger than you," I said. "And we're going to do everything we can to save her. But Vergil's our top-value target."

"And she can go hang?"

I resisted the urge to punch Mickey in the throat. "You think they would have hauled us out here to save just her?" I said. "We might have a lot more Spartans in the field these days, but we can't be everywhere. We can't save everyone."

Mickey grunted at me. "So she's just lucky she happened to get kidnapped along with a valuable alien."

Romeo shook his head. "I liked it better when we were shooting at the bugs instead of rescuing them."

"That's not the point," I said. Much as we'd been through, Romeo knew he grated on my nerves sometimes, and I'd started to think he liked it. "We got our orders, we got our fancy implants and armor, and so we get the job done."

"Aye-freaking-aye," Romeo said in as positive a tone as he could muster.

With that settled, or so I thought, we double-timed it up the sunny side of the mountain. None of us said another word. We'd worked together for too long to bother with small talk in the field.

That sort of thing had killed more soldiers than I care to think about. You started talking about your home life, such as it was, and you took your mind off the task at hand. The next thing you knew, enemy fire you never saw coming blew straight through your head.

We hadn't survived this many operations by letting ourselves get distracted. Besides which, we didn't always have that much to say to each other those days.

By the time we reached the ridge, the massive sun had fallen low, painting the sky in reds as dark as blood. The light amplifiers in my helmet automatically compensated for the encroaching dusk.

I gave the signal, and we crouched low. A little while later, we fell to our hands and knees and crawled the last several meters until we could peer down over the ridge, hoping no one spotted our helmets silhouetted against the darkening sunset.

A military base lay below us, nestled between two raised arms of the mountains and surrounded by low rock formations, along with a five o'clock shadow of scrub brush. It had been thrown together with prefabricated buildings that still bore UNSC logos.

Anywhere near civilization and the rebels would have taken the time to remove such markings to help hide their crimes, but out here in the wilds of this backwater colony, they hadn't bothered. They might even have worn the evidence of their thefts as a badge of honor.

Lights glowed throughout the complex, and people strolled between the buildings like they were relaxing at a resort rather than holing up with a stolen alien genius. A pair of banged-up transports squatted in a makeshift airfield that sprawled in the center of the buildings, and I spotted a last-gen fighter stuffed in a dusty hangar just beyond that.

It hadn't been loaded up with any ordnance, as far as I could see. Maybe they didn't have any. It might have been nothing more than a glorified high-speed taxi to them. Despite all that, they'd nabbed an Engineer right from under ONI's nose, which meant they had to be far more effective than their base's appearance implied.

Vergil could have done a lot to help get the place into shape, but from the looks of it, they hadn't dared let him that far off his leash yet. That reluctance wouldn't last forever though.

"What an ugly mess," Romeo said over our private comm channel. "What kind of idiots would put up with living in a hell-hole out in the sticks like this?"

"Idiots with a purpose," I said. "Rebels *with* a cause."

"They're not doing it for the ladies, Romes," said Mickey.

"That's Spartan Agu to you," Romeo said with a chuckle. "That's what all the girls call me."

"Cut the chatter." I'd focused on two people striding between a couple of the buildings, cutting across the airfield to save time. "This is an op, not a playground."

"Yes, sir, Spartan Buck, sir," Mickey said.

God, I wanted to smack him across the back of his helmet, but Romeo took care of that for me. Quietly, of course.

I scoped in on the pair. They looked like civilians out for an evening stroll—a man and a woman holding hands and chatting on their way to dinner. Watching them gave me a pang for Veronica, for a simpler life together that we'd probably never know. We could play at it in short bursts between missions, but we had our jobs.

And to be honest, our jobs had us.

My onboard operational database didn't match them with any of the Front leaders catalogued by ONI, but that didn't mean anything. The Front wasn't a combined force so much as an ideology, a creed to which overmilitarized colonists who didn't think they owed anything to the Unified Earth Government subscribed. While they didn't pose as much of a direct threat as whatever remained of the Covenant, their decentralization made them that much harder to kill.

We'd had the same trouble with the Covenant, of course. It's a lot easier to strike at the heart of a beast than to stomp out every bug in a hive.

I scoped down tighter on the couple. Maybe I let their apparent happiness out here in the ass-end of the galaxy distract me. They didn't look like they needed beaches or bars or shore leave or much of anything else they didn't have a hope of finding around here. They had each other, and I'll be damned if that didn't seem like plenty.

When the couple reached the center of the airfield, they veered toward the open hangar, and I saw a familiar blue glow move out to greet them. I brought the scope up just a bit and spotted an Engineer floating toward them. They waved to him, and I almost would have thought they were old friends but for the squad of armed guards that trailed in the alien's wake.

My HUD positively identified the Huragok as Vergil, and I allowed myself a smile. "Yup. That's the gasbag we're looking for," I said to the others.

I made to stand up but felt something hard jab me in the back of my helmet. "Hold it right there, Gunny," Romeo said over the comm channel. "Don't make one damn move. Please."

"What the hell?" I braced my arms to shove myself to my feet, and I got another knock in the back of the head for my efforts.

"Better listen to him, Buck," Mickey said. "Don't move a muscle." He sounded as grim as a medic telling a soldier that the only good thing about him bleeding out on the battlefield was that his cancer wouldn't get him first.

"Okay," I said. "This is an awful bad time for a joke."

A full platoon of heavily armed rebels emerged from the rock formations just below us. They'd been lying there, waiting for us the entire time and blending into the environment with their rust-colored armor. They fanned out quickly, keeping their weapons trained on us. My HUD now marked each and every one of them as a semicircle of red blips on my foe-finder.

"Gunny?" Romeo said. "I don't think anyone's laughing."

TWO

Hostage situations are never any fun.

As a Spartan, I'm trained to shoot enemies, not negotiate with them. The only language I'm fully fluent in is ordnance.

But I'd dealt with such troubles before. The last time was a year earlier, back in 2554, on my home planet of Draco III.

Yeah, that Draco III.

I wasn't a Spartan back then, obviously. But by the same token, I'd never say I was "just" an ODST, since that's something I'd aimed for my entire life up to that point.

Even though I grew up on Draco III, I hadn't been back there to visit my hometown of Karnak for years. The day I turned eighteen—August 25, 2528—I walked into the local UNSC recruiting office, stood there in line with everyone else who shared my birthday, and signed away my life to the Marines.

Before the Covenant had showed up in the human part of the galaxy three years prior to that birthday, the UNSC had spent most of its time putting down rebellions across colonial space, and I honestly hadn't thought much about joining the military. My mother had been a marine herself, but she gave it up to raise me and my kid sister, Lucy. And Dad had never wanted to be anything more than a dockworker and family man.

I never cared too much for school, and I spent my summers

apprenticing with my uncle Lou as a fisherman on the Gold Sea. Fish farms took care of filling most of Draco III's seafood demand, but Uncle Lou went after bigger game, the kind of tenacious critters that had been native to the planet before humanity terraformed it. These creatures survived by living far beneath the waves, but when they crept back up toward the surface, Lou and his compatriots went after them hard.

I still remember skimming along the ocean's surface on an industrial fishing ship, stalking a rare island-sized *naeori*. (That's the egghead name. Growing up, I always called them octowhales.)

You can't just blast the hell out of something like that. Regular munitions don't do more than simply annoy it—or worse, drive it back down into the deep. Bombs might work, but only by blasting the beast into parts small enough to be useless to anyone. So we had to herd the damn things into shocknets instead.

The nets used enough juice that they had to be attached to their own reactor, so you couldn't just drop them from above onto one of the creatures. You did that in waters too deep, and the octowhale would sink to the bottom before you could stop it. Then you were down not just the net and your chance at the cash that kind of rare sea creature catch can bring, but a whole reactor as well, and those things are pricey for someone on a sailor's salary.

On Draco III, fishing for big game like that was the closest thing we had to living like a cowboy back in Earth's Old West, centuries ago. And as much as the sea life stank and the salt stung, I loved the hell out of it. Out on those waves, far from the rest of even what Draco III called civilization, I felt free, like nothing could touch me. This was a life worth living for the rest of my days.

But in 2526, after I heard about humanity's violent first contact with the Covenant on the planet Harvest, I tossed those dreams aside. There was no other sane choice in my mind. I was underage at the time, but the first moment I could, I joined the Marines so I could help save my world, and the rest of humanity on top of it.

Of course, that didn't work out as well as I'd hoped.

I was in cryosleep between Mars and Hardscrabble in 2545, when the Covenant finally got around to invading Draco III. I was an old soldier by that point, about seventeen years on, and even though the UNSC tried to keep the news from the front lines just rosy for the folks at home, I knew the war wasn't going well for us. But I kept following orders and fighting my hardest, trusting in my superiors and doing my best to keep my nose clean between battles.

I'd been back to Draco III a few times on shore leave since I left, but extended stints in cryosleep meant the years zipped by my family far faster than they did for me. My parents got grayer every time I saw them, leaping closer toward retirement but still together and happy. Right up until my dad died in a traffic accident.

The last I saw of my sister, she was married with two kids, my nieces Cyan and Cho. I never had the opportunity to meet my nephew, Xu.

And then the Covenant came and killed them all.

I got the news as soon as I woke up on arrival at Hardscrabble. By then, every last human on Draco III had been murdered.

It felt like watching a history lesson about your own life, filling in a bit of backstory that had happened while you were sleeping the weeks away. Surreal, shocking, and saddening all at once.

I don't know exactly what happened to my family, but I can only hope they went fast, in the initial assault. That's what happened to the lucky ones, before things turned absolutely terrifying planetside.

Once the Covenant beat Draco III's defenses into dust, they sent Grunts and Jackals down to the surface for some R&R. In this case, that stood for Round-up and Rub-out. I heard they hunted down the human survivors for sport and then cackled themselves silly as they ate them and gnawed on their raw, bloody bones.

I was encouraged to not watch the videos. "You don't need that kind of shit floating around in your head," my old sergeant told me.

But I couldn't stop myself. I had to see what had happened, what the Covenant had done. I became obsessed with watching every last second that I could find. And when I was done, I went back and sat through it all again.

I wanted to know who we were fighting and what horrors they could do. I wanted to burn those atrocities into my brain until they filled my dreams. I wanted to make sure I'd never forget what we were up against and why we had to give everything to the fight.

Everything the bastards hadn't already taken from us.

The UNSC sent Spartans to Draco III to fight the Covenant, but they arrived way too late to do any of the people there any good. They couldn't save anyone—only avenge them.

Everyone else might have cheered at the images of humanity's superheroes diving in and kicking some Covenant ass, but all I could think about was how useless it was to pin our hopes on a few handfuls of super-soldiers who couldn't possibly be everywhere we needed them to be.

After all, how much good had they done for my mom? Or Lucy and her kids?

It was then that I put in for an immediate transfer to the ODSTs. *That's* where I figured I could get things done fastest and do the most good.

Someone in High Command must have been taking pity on the soldiers who hailed from Draco III. I got my new orders just a few weeks later, which, when it comes to the UNSC, seems like lightspeed.

And I made the best I could out of that opportunity. I fought those Covenant bastards like hell and gave them everything I had.

THREE

After the Covenant War ended late in 2552, a few groups of displaced humans decided to try to resettle Draco III. Miraculously, because the Covenant had saved the planet as a hunting ground for its worst scum to enjoy, most of the place hadn't been glassed. That didn't mean the cities were open for business and ready for people to occupy, but it's a lot easier to clean up a place than to have to rebuild it from scratch.

Me though? I hadn't gone back. I'd already taken out as much grief on the Covenant as I cared to, and there obviously wasn't any home left for me to return to. It would have been as useful as visiting a gravesite.

Plus, I still had other battles left to fight.

The Unified Earth Government also had more items on its agenda than trying to dictate who settled where. No matter how the United Rebel Front or any of the other splinter groups liked to paint it, the UEG mostly left them alone—as long as they behaved. It wasn't until the Front did something stupid like trying to violently secede an entire planet from the UEG that they demanded the UNSC's attention—and sure as hell got it.

The stupidity filtered over to Draco III not too long after the resettlement began. The rebel leaders on my homeworld decided that they needed to act fast to declare the planet independent, before too many reasonable settlers arrived. That, of course, didn't sit well with the decent people who had already set up shop there, or with the Office of Naval Intelligence, which focused on Draco III's strategic importance as the UEG moved to reclaim many of the lost colonies that lay beyond it.

"That's why you're the right man for the job," Veronica had told me. "You're one of the few Draco natives left—and the only one in the ODSTs."

"Why don't you just let the Spartans handle it?" I asked. "You've got a whole new bunch of them who I'm sure are looking for things to blow holes into."

"ONI prefers not to use blunt instruments where a scalpel would be better," she said, though we both knew it had more to do with cost than efficiency.

"Come on. You can't reason with the Front," I said. "They're not interested in anything but their own way."

"We're just hoping you and the rest of Alpha-Nine can keep a cap on the collateral damage."

I smiled at that. "You know, you look a lot like Veronica Dare, but you must be a shapeshifting spy. The real Veronica knows better than to claim my ODST fireteam would cause less damage on an op than any other choice."

She patted me on the cheek. "Look. The sight of Spartans puts the rebels into a frenzy. They think of them as the symbol of all that's wrong with the UEG. They call them fascist super-soldiers and claim they'll eventually take over humanity in a military coup that will spell the end for regular folks everywhere."

"And are they wrong about that?"

"Well, soldier, I'm afraid that's classified."

"And far above my pay grade either way."

"By your own choice." I could hear the accusation in her voice.

"Ah. I didn't think you went for overengineered post-humans like that."

"They came to you with the offer, Eddie."

"Wait. I never told you that."

"It's my business to know things."

"Well, then you should know why I turned them down."

"Because you're a stubborn ass."

"But I'm *your* stubborn ass."

"For now, anyway."

But I found that being stubborn wasn't enough. Not on that day, at least.

I should have just given in to Veronica. She always got her way when it came to me, and her request that I lead my team back to Draco III didn't prove any exception.

It wasn't just my natural orneriness that kept me from wanting to be a good little soldier when it came to that particular job though. Well, that was some of it, sure, but the fact was I just didn't want to return to the scene of one of the Covenant's worst crimes. I've seen all sorts of horrible things in my career—things that would make you want to weep tears of blood—but Draco III was personal. I didn't want to spend every second on that familiar old ball of dirt seething with righteous fury.

Since the end of the war, I'd had this satisfying sense of accomplishment, that when it came to stopping the Covenant invasion at least, we'd done what we set out to do. It felt healthy, and I wanted that to be enough for me. I worried that going back to Draco III would reopen the wounds I'd worked so hard to heal.

But I'd never let fear stop me before. I wouldn't be much of a soldier if I did.

You follow your orders. You do your job. Every damn time.

So I went back to Draco III in 2554, and I took the rest of Alpha-Nine with me.

FOUR

espite ONI's preferences, my team gave up on the subtle approach soon after we hit Draco III. The rebels who had taken over the capitol building in the heart of New Albany didn't respond well to much other than bullets. ONI wanted us to take down their leadership, but the determined little bastards had—probably not coincidentally—barricaded themselves inside the best-built structure on the planet.

Nothing short of a nuke from the air would be able to dislodge them from the capitol building, and I was fresh out of that kind of ordnance. Besides which, we had orders to leave the area as intact as possible. If we'd gone in and brought the building down on top of the rebel leaders' heads, that would have only given the rest of the Front a crater to rally around where the heart of the city had stood. The last thing ONI needed was to give the Front's propaganda machine a new recruiting tool: *See how the UEG treats you when you object to their iron-fisted rule?*

So instead, we got dropped inside the Front's perimeter and stormed the capitol on foot. Back then, there were five of us in Alpha-Nine: me, Dutch, Romeo, Mickey, and the Rookie.

We fought well and made good headway toward the rebel leader, a woman who called herself Captain Ingridson.

And then they cornered us hard.

We got all the way to the floor of Draco III's old legislature, which the rebels had commandeered as their headquarters. Using explosives, we punched through into the room where Draco's laws had been formed, debated, and passed, only to find the place empty.

It was a trap. As soon as we got inside, they closed off the way behind us.

I spotted a way out through an emergency door, and I sent the Rookie to go for it while the rest of us covered him. Damn kid did a great job, dodging from cover to cover, and he made it to the exit in no time.

His job from there was to circle around behind the rebels who were keeping the rest of us trapped in the room. With luck, he'd catch them by surprise and take them out before they knew he was coming. At the very least, he'd distract them enough to give the rest of Alpha-Nine a chance to blast back past them and out into the open again.

The next time we saw the Rookie, though, he was a bloody mess. He'd been shot in the shoulder and beaten bloody, and he'd lost his helmet somewhere along the way. A couple of soldiers dragged him up onto the balcony at the front of the legislative chambers—the one from which the Draco III president used to address the planet—and presented him to us. We dove straight for cover and tried to figure out our next move.

Well, *I* tried, anyway. The others were never that great at coming up with plans on the fly. But that's why I outranked them.

I was still strategizing when Captain Ingridson herself appeared next to the Rookie and pressed a pistol barrel flat against his temple. I signaled the others to press back and hide.

"Stand down, imperialists!" she shouted. The Rookie tried to angle his head out of the way, but the rebels holding his arms had him in a vicious grip. "Give yourselves up now, or your comrade dies!"

The rebels had us goddamn good, and they knew it. After an assassination attempt in the days before the Covenant War, the presidential balcony had been protected from just about any kind of attack. There was no way anything we had with us could penetrate the transparent energy shielding around it—not without killing the Rookie as well.

"Just say the word, Gunny." Romeo hefted a string of grenades in his hand. "I can take them all out."

"Not with those, you can't," said Dutch.

"I don't have to hit them," said Romeo. "Just get close enough to blow the moorings out from under that balcony."

"And you kill the Rookie, too," Mickey said.

"He knew what he was signing up for," Romeo said. "We all did, right?"

I couldn't argue with Romeo's stunted logic. Trading the Rookie for Captain Ingridson would put an end to the rebellion on Draco III—but only for a few days, at best, until someone new occupied the power vacuum.

I just couldn't bring myself to let the kid get killed like that. Not without trying to save him. We'd been through too damn much together for me to cut him loose. That's when a sharp voice sliced into my comm system and presented a new option I didn't really want. "Gunnery Sergeant Buck? This is Spartan Sarah Palmer. I understand you're having some problems. We're here to help."

FIVE

I recognized Palmer's voice at once. They tell you that the UNSC is huge, and they're not joking. Still, when you're talking about elite soldiers like those in the ODST, that's a much smaller number. We don't all know each other, but most of the time there's only a degree or two of separation between us at most.

With me and Sarah Palmer, that degree was zero.

Back in 2546, Palmer and her own ODST group, Gamma-Six, wound up getting sent into Belisk, a town built around a number of large-scale manufacturing plants belonging to Lethbridge Industrial on the colony planet Sargasso. The Covenant had assaulted the planet, and we were giving it to them good in the sky. But nevertheless, the bugs had sent a ground force down to destroy Belisk and cripple its production facilities.

I didn't know it at the time, but Lethbridge was chest-deep in manufacturing all sorts of military-grade gear and munitions for the UNSC in general, and ONI in particular. ONI had invested a mountain of money in Belisk for all that gear, and it was up to Gamma-Six to protect that investment in the most aggressive way.

Little did Sarah Palmer know, though, that ONI didn't like to take chances when it came to such large investments. They gathered up my Alpha-Nine team and ordered us in at the same time, but with a different mission. While Gamma-Six was supposed to protect the facility, it was our job to grab all of Lethbridge's latest research data before it could fall into Covenant hands.

The Cole Protocol dictated that any kind of data that might lead the Covenant toward Earth had to be wiped out if there was any chance it could fall into enemy hands, but that emergency order didn't strictly apply to other bits of data that were marginally less vital. ONI hated to let hard-earned research and development go to waste if they could help it, so we were sent in to secure the data and guarantee its safe passage to Concord, the colony where Lethbridge Industrial was originally based.

It wasn't like the Covenant could outfit the Elites in UNSC gear. Our helmets wouldn't fit around their ugly heads, for one. But on the other hand, ONI didn't want the Covenant to know anything more about our cutting-edge equipment and research than they could figure out by prying it off a fallen trooper who'd been doing his best to kill them.

"I don't like this at all," I told our ONI liaison, none other than Captain Veronica Dare herself.

I'd met Veronica for the first time a year earlier than that, when I was on shore leave back in 2545. Looking back, it's hard to believe we've known each other that long, but spending months traveling through the stars in cryosleep really makes those years fly by.

The Covenant had destroyed Draco III earlier that year, and my CO at the time had ordered me to take some shore leave I didn't really want to have. She'd tossed a few phrases at me like "taking too many risks," "jeopardizing others," and "mental health break," which I did my best to ignore. It wasn't until she threatened to send me for a psychiatric evaluation that I finally gave in.

We met in a swim-up bar in a zero-G resort in Castellaneta, a tourist station set in geosynchronous orbit on the sunny side of Saturn's outermost ring. Most people just came there to float around and enjoy the overpriced drinks, but I got this huge kick out of the weightlessness. I've gone without gravity lots of times, of course, but it's different when you're on duty.

I remember the first time I saw Veronica. She was standing alone in the middle of the club in a long silver skirt, glittering like diamonds in the morning sun. I knew right then she was exactly what I needed to get my mind off Draco III.

I'd like to tell you that we spent weeks getting to know each other. That we took it slow and let our relationship build. But that would be bullshit.

We were soldiers taking some well-earned time off in the middle of a war over the fate of our entire people. We didn't fall into each other's arms. We jumped.

It didn't end with that one night though. We spent an entire week together and made the most of every damn moment.

I'd never met anyone like her. Smart, confident, beautiful, and ready to take me on every level. Oh, she had my number—hell, I *gave* it to her—and I worked as hard as I could to find hers.

I just didn't have any idea what she was hiding behind it. It wasn't until our week careened to an end that I figured it out.

Okay, I didn't actually figure it out. She had to paint it on the wall for me.

We were lying in bed, entangled in each other's arms. I had to catch the next transport out of the resort, and I knew she wasn't long for there either.

"Does this have to end?" I asked.

I felt her tense up against me, and I knew the answer before she could open her lips. I hoped, though, that it might just be her

— 23 —

reflexes betraying her. The smart thing would have been for me to let it go right there—to let *her* go—but I couldn't bring myself to do it.

"I don't mean to push you—" I started.

"Yes, you do." She gazed up into my eyes, her head nestled on my shoulder, and I couldn't find a way to argue with her about it. "And I want you to. I just don't know if I can let you."

That broke the spell for me, and I cocked my head down at her. "Is there someone else?"

Her chuckle told me that wasn't the problem.

"Because if there is," I said, "I can take care of that for you. I am a trained professional, after all."

"And a crack shot from a thousand meters." Her tender mouth formed a gentle smile.

It wasn't what she said so much as how she said it. I *am* a crack shot, and I made top marks in sniper school to prove it. She wasn't just taking my word for my skills and making a joke about it. She said it like she knew my exact score.

I narrowed my eyes at her, and her smile vanished. She pushed herself out of the bed and started to get dressed.

"Hey, what the hell?" I asked in as mannered a way as I could manage.

She didn't look at me.

"Veronica—what's going on here?" I got up and started slipping into my clothes, too.

"I can't tell you," she said.

"What's that supposed to mean?"

"Just what I said. I haven't lied to you. Not once."

"But you haven't told me the whole truth, have you?" I sized her up in a way I hadn't bothered to before—not as a potential date but as a threat. "What aren't you telling me?"

"Don't ask me that." She pleaded at me with her bright blue eyes. *Don't ruin what we just had*, they said. *Just let us treasure this precious moment for everything it was, and nothing more.*

But I couldn't help it. "Who are you . . . ? Really?"

She finished dressing and started for the door. I knew six ways to stop her, but they all leaped into my head out of my military training. None of them would work here, not the way I wanted them to, and I felt as helpless as if I'd been shot through the heart.

"Is Veronica even your real name?"

She stopped at the door and glared back at me, her eyes bluer than ever and glittering with fought-back tears.

"Stupidly enough, yes," she said. "And I shouldn't have shared."

That's when I figured it out. My eyes must've grown as large as spotlights. "Ah hell. You're a goddamn spook!"

She frowned. "I work for ONI, and I shouldn't have even told you that. We're on the same side."

"Are you here on a job? Whoa"—I stabbed a finger into my chest—"am *I* your job?"

The dead-eyed look she speared me with told me I'd nailed it. "My job has nothing to do with this."

"How the hell am I supposed to believe that?" I clapped my forehead in disbelief. "You just admitted to being a professional liar."

"I haven't lied to you."

"Yet."

She pushed past me and put her hand on the door, but she stopped there and stared back at me. Her eyes burned with regret. "It didn't have to end like this."

Maybe I wasn't being fair to her. Maybe I was being a massive jackass. Or maybe I was right.

I'll note that those three things aren't mutually exclusive.

At that moment, though, I didn't damn well care. I only knew I didn't want her to walk out that door.

"Look." I held an open hand out to her. "I'm sorry. We were having such a good time, and I never wanted it to end. And you—"

She arched a thin eyebrow at me, daring me to say something wrong.

I took a deep breath and said the most honest thing I could. "You took me by surprise."

"Funny," she said, her words as cold as space. "You didn't surprise me at all."

SIX

I didn't know if I'd ever see Veronica again after that week.

I managed to track her down through UNSC channels, but she ignored me every time I tried to initiate contact. She didn't say one word to me for almost a year.

If she hadn't been the ONI agent in charge of the operations on Sargasso in 2546, we might have managed to miss each other forever. Even so, when she came to deliver my team's briefing personally, she acted like she barely knew me. When I told her I didn't like Alpha-Nine's assignment to rescue Lethbridge tech from Sargasso, she discarded my opinion out of hand.

"You're not required to like it," Veronica said. She was so cool and professional about it, I wondered for a second if I'd once had such a great time with her twin sister instead. "You just need to follow your orders and get the job done."

"But I don't *get* it." I nodded at Samrat, the ODST I'd served with longest at that point, and he shrugged in agreement. He didn't understand the assignment either, but he wasn't about to argue with an ONI officer about it.

Me, I wanted to survive it if I could. Even at that point in my career, I'd already been sent on enough suicide missions. As a matter of fact, I was working with an entirely different fireteam back then, not one of whom is still breathing today.

That's the nature of war, I'm afraid. It's rare for a team to be able to remain whole for long. Back then, Alpha-Nine consisted of me, Samrat, Svensdottir, and Gomez.

You might notice I'm the only one still on that list.

They were good soldiers, one and all, and each of them deserved to live toward a long and peaceful retirement. The best I can say for them is that they died well.

I can only hope to manage the same when my time comes.

At that moment, though, I had to deal with taking orders from someone who didn't seem to like me much at all.

Veronica gave me the kind of exasperated sigh I'd only heard from people who had real issues with me, and then she slowly repeated herself.

"You need to find a way into the Lethbridge facility. Make your way to the main lab." She paused to make sure I was still following her. I gestured for her to go on. "And then confiscate the central data chip all the engineers who worked there kept loaded with the results of their years of irreplaceable research. What's so hard to understand about that?"

"The part where we have to find our way into the facility," I said.

"Right," Gomez said. "Why don't we just drop down on top of it?"

"Discretion is vital here." Veronica set her jaw and sized us up. She didn't trust any one of us—least of all, me—not yet. In that sense, at least, she was ONI all the way. But she decided she had to let one last bit of information drop. "The UNSC isn't aware of your mission."

I shot the rest of the troops an *I-told-you-so* look. Svensdottir threw up her hands in disgust. "But there's another ODST team going in ahead of us. Gamma-Six doesn't know either?"

"If the UNSC knew about your target, they'd engage in standard operating procedure."

I narrowed my eyes at her. "And you don't want that because . . . ?"

Veronica looked like she might spit blood. "They'd encircle the lab and dig in. You might as well paint a bull's-eye on the place and let the Covenant know where to hit us hardest."

Samrat groaned in realization. "So Gamma-Six is there to distract the Covenant from the real target."

I liked it now even less. "And you expect them to die doing that."

"Battle analysis from our AI shows that this is the only real chance we have to recover that data and those prototypes and keep them out of Covenant hands. Without the other team's mission, your chance of success drops precipitously."

"All right," I said with an exaggerated shrug. "We'll do it your way."

"You don't have any other choice."

"Of course not," I said in a low voice as I brushed past her, leading the Alpha-Nine team toward the transport that Veronica already had waiting for us. "But that doesn't mean you have to be rude about it."

She didn't buy my hurt-feelings act for even as long as it took us to gather our gear and get on the transport. She caught up with us just as I ushered the last of my teammates onto the dropship and grabbed me by the elbow. "This is more important than you could know."

"You mean, than I'm *allowed* to know." I glanced down at my arm, and she released it. "Oh, so we're actually talking now . . . ? Look, I'm well aware of how ONI plays soldiers like pieces on a game board. Just don't expect me to like it."

"I value the lives of every one of your soldiers just as much as you do."

"Uh-huh. I seriously doubt that."

"I know you don't trust ONI. I get it. I wouldn't respect you if you did."

"Respect? I'm an old-fashioned kind of guy, and I think you're moving just a little too fast."

She bit back a response that might have blown my head off. "Buck. We run the numbers. We slice the scenarios every way we can. We do the goddamn math. We don't risk anyone on our side unless we know the data's on our side, too."

The transport's engines fired up then, and I leaned down close to speak into her ear. "That's the difference between us," I said. "I only care about the *people* on my side."

I left her standing there on the transport pad, and right then I figured I'd never see her again. Either I'd get myself killed on her high-risk mission, or she'd find someone easier to work with the next time around. I couldn't let that or the look in those bright blue eyes of hers bother me then though. If I wanted me and the rest of Alpha-Nine to survive, I had to focus instead on the craptastic mission she'd handed us.

The transport dropped us off five klicks outside of Belisk. After enough whining about sore legs from Gomez, I had Svensdottir hotwire an abandoned civilian truck with the Lethbridge Industrial logo emblazoned on the side. The rest of us piled in the truck's cargo bay and tried not to get knocked around too much as she gunned her way through town.

"Slow down!" I shouted over the comm. "The whole point here is to not get noticed!"

"I'm the only truck on the inbound highway," she said. "What the hell do you expect me to do?"

"We're on a stealth mission," I said. "Drive stealthily!"

To her credit, Svensdottir only snickered at that for a couple seconds before she pretended to try to humor me. She wove her way through Belisk's abandoned, shell-shattered streets until we reached Lethbridge's main facility, screeching to a halt fast enough to make me feel like I might catapult through the truck's front wall.

"Shit," she said. "Incoming!"

Gomez, Samrat, and I were already heading for the rear cargo doors when Svensdottir stomped on the accelerator again. The doors splayed open before us, and our momentum sent us sailing out the back to land sprawling on the street beyond.

I turned around just in time to see the missile Svensdottir had been trying to avoid smacking into the back of the truck and detonating in a gigantic ball of fire. Svensdottir spilled out of the driver's side door, howling the entire way. But thankfully it was more of a war whoop than a cry of pain. She was okay for the moment.

I rolled to my feet, unlimbering my battle rifle. "Target's at three o'clock high," I said. "Sam! Scoot right and concentrate fire on him! Gogo! You put Daughter's fire out! Haul her behind the truck until we send this bastard to hell!"

To their eternal credit, my team did exactly as ordered. We pay a lot of lip service to that in the Marines—especially with the ODSTs—but you don't realize how much of a difference that makes until someone screws it up. Alpha-Nine was a well-oiled machine.

Of course, war blasts even the best machines to pieces.

As Sam moved to the right and forced our attackers to keep their heads down—at least for as long as it took them to reload their fuel-rod gun—I went to the left to split any incoming fire. As I did, I plucked a grenade from my belt and thumbed it active. The Covenant bastards were chattering at us from a balcony overlooking the entrance to the Lethbridge headquarters, so I overarmed the charge at them in a high arc.

The grenade went off an instant after it landed, blasting out all the windows from the balcony and sending a pair of Grunts sailing over the railing, too. Somewhere up there, an Elite bellowed in pain and then collapsed with a heavy thud.

As far as I'm concerned, that's one of the sweetest sounds in the galaxy.

"So much for the stealthy approach!" Sam said while my ears were still ringing.

"I never cared for that ONI bullshit, anyway." I signaled for Sam to cover me as I charged up the open steps and then kicked the spiderwebbed safety glass out of one of the doors. No one challenged me.

I scanned the foyer. "Clear! Gogo, report!"

"Daughter's good as gold, Gunny," he said. I glanced back to see him hustling Svensdottir to join up with me while Sam covered our backs.

"Feel like I got scorched that color," Svensdottir said as she shoved aside the pain. She huffed hard but didn't limp a lick.

Despite our noisy entrance, we only found token resistance once we pushed into the complex. Much as I hated to admit it, ONI's plan worked like a bullet through butter. Just no stopping it.

I wasn't one to question our blessings, so we pushed toward the lab hard and fast. I knew it wouldn't take much for the Covenant commanders in the area to turn their attention toward us, but by the time that happened, I planned to have Alpha-Nine long gone. Also, some small part of me hoped that we could be done with it all fast enough to make a difference for the troopers in Gamma-Six. Once we wrapped up our job, Command could order them out.

"Gogo, you're on the point. Daughter, cover my left. Sam, you watch our six." I didn't really need to say the words. That was our standard formation, and we'd used it dozens of times in situations just like this.

The ritual of it, though, felt right. I'm not superstitious, but I take comfort on the battlefield in following the patterns I've drilled into my team's heads. It makes you feel like you have some kind of control in even the least controlled places, and when you have bullets flying all around you, that helps stave off any panic.

We moved through the halls as fast as we could, clearing side rooms with a glance, just to make sure no bugs would slide up behind us. We kept quiet, whispering into our comms rather than shouting.

We took the stairs up to the fourth floor rather than risk the elevator. Nothing like an arrival bell to let anyone in the area know you're there and when they can start shooting you, after all. When we got there, Gogo breached the door, and Daughter and I covered him, me going high while she went low.

We found a squad of Brutes and Grunts waiting there in the foyer for us, their weapons all at the ready and trained on the elevator doors straight across from us. If we'd have done things the easy way, they'd have loaded the elevator car with plasma bursts and grenades before we'd even been able to step out of it. As it was, we caught them flat-footed.

Gogo, Daughter, and I unloaded a full clip each into the bastards, and the Covenant soldiers either dove for what little cover they could find—like behind one another—or died. The three of us swung back into the stairwell to reload, and Sam pitched a grenade straight past me to land right in the middle of the room. It went off just as the survivors started to poke their heads up to see where we'd gone.

It was like poetry.

We strolled past the dead aliens and shoved our way through the lab's shattered doors. "Did my little popper do all that?" Samrat asked as he gaped at the destruction.

I shook my head and frowned. "These guys were hard at work trashing this place before we showed up."

"Did they perhaps already get the thing for which we came here?" said Svensdottir.

"Let's hope not." I glanced around and made a few quick decisions. "We don't need all of us to ransack this place, but we are going to need another ride out of here once we find it. Gogo? Go see what kind of wheels you can find us."

"On it, Gunny," he said with a sharp nod.

"Sam, keep a watch on the foyer here while Daughter and I work the janitorial duty and toss the room for our data chip. I don't want anyone sneaking up on us while our attention's away."

"On it."

"I could help Gogo find us transportation," Svensdottir said.

"He's as sneaky as they come." I turned on my comm to make sure he'd hear my next words. "He won't take any stupid chances out there on his own."

"Never have, Gunny," he said. "Never will."

I glanced at Svensdottir, then jerked my head in the direction Gomez had gone. She took off after him like I'd dropped a hot bullet casing down her back.

I rummaged around the trashed labs and didn't see anything obvious, like a glowing pedestal upon which a diamond-crusted chip sat sparkling in a spotlight. I did locate a central computer interface, but it looked like the Grunts had given it a rubdown with their pistols. The slot where the data chip would have gone stood empty.

I switched my comm off, cursing. I cocked my head at the slot and gave it a closer look. It didn't seem like the Grunts had bashed in that particular part of the console, and I didn't see half of a broken chip still stuck in the slot. That meant it had to be around there somewhere.

I scoured the place, fast. If one of the lab techs had hidden it, I could have spent hours there trying to find it. A chip like that's not any bigger than a poker card. You could slip it anywhere.

Most of the lab sat in one large room filled with stations, tables, and cubicles. A single door, though, led into a glassed-off area that featured a desk and a great view of the complex's inner courtyard. The interior glass and the exterior windows had all been shattered, and I could hear bursts of plasma fire off in the distance, just a bit every half minute or so. No screams sounded out in response.

The desk had been shot all to hell. It had lost so much of its structure that it actually sagged in the middle. I walked around behind it and found a middle-aged woman in a bloodstained lab coat hiding behind it. All the life had leaked out of her, turning her white coat red.

I knelt down next to her and closed her eyes. Then I muttered an apology as I patted down her pockets. I didn't like having to do it, but if she'd died trying to protect that data chip, then I'd have dishonored her efforts if I decided that rummaging through her clothing would be disrespectful.

I found the chip in the pocket of her lab coat.

"Got it," I said over the comm as I slipped the chip into my armor's hardcase. "Find us a taxi yet, Gogo?"

"On my way back, Gunny! Meet you at the front door!"

Before I left, I grabbed a grenade and tossed it far across the inner courtyard. It bounced off a window on the other side and exploded in midair, shattering every bit of glass around it.

"Do we have company?" Svensdottir asked over the comm.

"Just a little manufactured distraction," I told her. "But I do hope that's what any Covie in the area thinks."

Sam and I double-timed it down the stairs and toward the way we'd come in. Svensdottir stopped us halfway through the foyer. I had just enough time to ask "What's up?" before the back of a flatbed trailer came smashing through what was left of the building's front doors.

"You know Gogo," Svensdottir said. "Loves to make an entrance."

"Por supuesto!" Gomez leaned out the driver's side window of the truck he'd commandeered and waved us on. "Climb aboard!"

Sam eyeballed the truck. "Where are we supposed to sit?"

"Daughter, you take shotgun," I said.

"And us?" said Sam.

I pointed to a tarp covering a load of bricks on the flatbed. "We're going incognito."

Sam grumbled as we slipped under the tarp and shoved aside enough bricks to make room for our armored butts. "I don't think this meets UNSC safety regs," he said. "Where are the seat belts?"

"You can file a complaint when you get home. Which you should manage nicely if I don't knock you off onto the highway." I tore a hole through the tarp, wide enough to see through. "Meanwhile, try to enjoy the view."

Gomez barreled the truck onto the nearest open road, moving fast enough for me to question my judgment as much as Sam had. He headed straight for our extraction point, where Veronica had promised she'd have a transport waiting to fly us and her grocery order home.

I couldn't get Gamma-Six out of my head, though, so I decided to listen in on their comm chatter. While Alpha-Nine had gone in using an encoded channel, per our operation's orders, Gamma-Six's frequency lay open to other ODST personnel, and I took full advantage of that.

My ears rang immediately with bangs and screams, and it took me a moment to make out a woman shouting orders over it all. "Keep going!" she barked at her people. "Head for the gate!"

Then she bellowed at Command. "Where the hell's our ride out of here, dammit?"

"Hold on," Command replied. "We're getting some interference on your vitals signals. What's Sergeant Pham's condition?"

"On her way to meet her ancestors," the woman said. "I'm next in line, so talk to *me*! *Now!*"

"It's too hot over your position, Lance Corporal Palmer," Command responded in a voice so calm you knew the speaker had his ass surgically planted in a comfy chair. "You need to extricate yourself to a safe location before we can send the transport in."

I brought up Gamma-Six's position on my HUD. They were hunkered down about three klicks from us, surrounded by Covenant soldiers and running out of options fast. A scream of agony pierced my eardrum over the comm. On my HUD, one of the blue lights indicating a friendly fighter snuffed out like a candle in a hurricane.

"We're dying out here!" Palmer shouted. "They have a flock of Banshees pinning us down!"

"I repeat—"

I shouldn't have cut Command off, but I had a healthy lack of respect for such manners. "Gamma-Six, this is Alpha-Nine. We are in your vicinity and are heading in your direction."

I fed the new destination to Gomez's HUD and smiled as I felt the speeding truck lurch in that direction.

"Alpha-Nine . . . ?" Command sounded like I'd pissed in his

beer. "This channel's been reserved for Gamma-Six. You're not a part of this operation!"

"Well, we are now. ODSTs don't leave each other behind."

Command grunted, and then a familiar and far more passionate voice growled at me over the comm. "Alpha-Nine? Your orders are clear. You are to return to the LZ and rendezvous with your transport without delay."

Veronica Dare could make a prison guard wet his trunks, but I ignored her. "Our current path will take us right to Gamma-Six's position. We picked up your MacGuffin, and if you want it home safe, I recommend you send our ride in that direction."

"I'm giving you a direct order."

I grimaced and gave my next words more thought than I usually bother with. "Command, I could pretend that you're breaking up, but I'd rather not insult you."

"Thank you." Her tone grew more even, but sharper, like a saw transforming into a razor.

"We're going to see if we can do Gamma-Six some good, and if you have a problem with that, you can take it up with UNSC High Command. I'm pretty sure my real bosses will have my back."

"Honestly?" The suspicious curl of her voice made me doubt my name, rank, and serial number. "How's that?"

"Because we're covering Gamma-Six's back. That's what marines do."

Veronica then taught me a few new ways to question someone's bloodline. I just tuned her out until she gave up in disgust.

By the time we got near Gamma-Six, all but one of the team's blue lights had gone out. To their credit, not one of my teammates questioned my judgment the entire way, even as we watched those lights fade one by one. Gomez gunned the engine harder instead.

"I'm solo here," Palmer said through the comm. "Just ran out of ammo, too."

For someone in such trouble, she exuded serenity. However her day might end, she stood ready to see it through. I wasn't about to leave her to die.

"Gogo!" I barked. "Dump us off a few meters from what's left of Gamma-Six! Daughter! Give me and Sam some cover! We're going in!"

As we reached the plaza in which Gamma-Six had been pinned down, Gomez spotted the Covenant forces massed across the street before us. "Hold on!" he said. "They got their backs to us, and I'm gonna make them hurt for it!"

A trio of Brutes stood there in the center of the street, directing a dozen Grunts and a half-dozen Jackals in their squad, who had fanned out in a semicircle around Palmer's position. A pair of Banshees spiraled overhead, hunting for any stray members of Gamma-Six who might try to make a break for it. Soon enough, the Grunts would gather their courage—or the Brutes would beat it into them—and they'd charge straight at Palmer. I had no doubt she'd fight them to her dying breath, but those weren't good odds for anyone.

Until we showed up to even them.

Gomez gunned that big rig right toward the Brutes and then yanked the wheel to the left at the last second. The truck spun sideways, sweeping into the Brutes and their Jackal scouts like a gigantic broom.

As the truck screeched to a blood-splattered halt, I tore off the tarp, and Samrat and I leaped off the flatbed. We dashed in the direction where Palmer's light still shone blue on my HUD while Svensdottir rained down suppressive fire with her assault rifle.

I peppered the two standing Jackals with my battle rifle, and they fell over like I'd snipped their strings. Sam cut wide to the right and kept the remaining Grunts busy while I made a beeline for Palmer.

By the time I reached Palmer—who'd taken cover in a shattered storefront—she'd already thrown one of her teammates over her shoulders and was starting toward me. She was covered with blood, and for her sake I could only hope it belonged to him.

"Grab the other two?" she said to me.

I wanted to charge straight past her without a nod, but the Banshees had spotted us. One of them opened fire on the cab of the truck while the other spun toward Samrat.

Sam never shied away from a fair fight, but he knew the Banshee had him outgunned. He hunkered down behind a blown-out car and called for help.

"We're kind of busy here!" Gomez shouted. The truck had stalled out after smashing into the Brutes, and it refused to start right back up again. He kept coaxing at it just the same while Svensdottir maintained a barrage of fire aimed at making them a harder target for the Banshee locked on them.

"Put him down." I tossed Palmer an ammo clip, and she caught it with her free hand. "We gotta live through this before we can think about our dead."

I didn't wait to see what she did. Instead, I spun around, dropped to one knee, and drew a bead on the Banshee circling around Sam's position.

"Why the hell are you hiding behind such a beat-up car?" I asked as the Banshee strafed Sam. The Elite piloting it bellowed down at him in triumph.

"I figured they couldn't blow up the gas in it twice!" he howled in some crazed mixture of fear, agony, and frustration. "You going to help me live to regret that decision, or what?"

I squeezed off a burst of bullets that lit up the energy field around the Elite pilot's armor. That got his attention, but he seemed baffled for a moment as to where the bullets could be coming from. The Sangheili had expected them from the marine he'd been attacking, and in a strategic error, he put his back to me.

The Banshee curled around to its pilot's right, giving me a clear shot at him from behind. Rather than unload everything I had, I lined up the crosshairs in my scope on his vitals and put a few solid bursts into them. I don't know if that killed him or not, but it knocked his shields out and dropped him from the cockpit. The fall finished him off either way, and the Banshee sailed off without him, straight into a building's facade.

While Sam cheered me on, I pulled back from my sights to see if I could spot the remaining Banshee going after Gomez and Svensdottir. Palmer was already on it. She'd loaded the clip I gave her into a battle rifle of her own, and she'd charged out into the plaza to draw fire from our ride.

"Sam!" I said. "Mop up the rest of those Grunts out there and haul ass back to the rig!"

Gomez finally got the truck's engine purring again, and he slammed it into reverse to drag it off the Brutes he'd crushed under its tires. He pulled back just in time to avoid another strafing run from the second Banshee. As it passed over the spot where the truck had been, Svensdottir lit it up with her assault rifle.

The Banshee was already smoking, and that last round of bullets set the machine on fire. The Elite piloting it, though, wasn't ready to give up and go home quite yet. He'd spotted what I'd done to his wingman—creature, whatever—and he veered straight for me. If he was going to die here, he planned to take me out with him at least.

Palmer stepped out from behind a lamppost she'd been using for cover, and she let loose at the Banshee with every last round in her magazine. About halfway through those slugs, the Banshee went up in a fiery blast, but she kept shooting anyway, just to make sure.

Given how those aliens had chewed up the rest of her squad, I couldn't blame her.

Palmer tossed the weapon aside and came back to pick up the fallen soldier she'd been carrying when I first saw her. "Help me with the others?" she said.

I clapped her outstretched hand. "This bus isn't leaving anyone behind."

I waved Sam over and stabbed a finger down at the next downed ODST I saw. While he scooted over and scooped that one up, I tracked down the last of the KIAs.

There wasn't a lot left of him. He had more spikes from one of those Brute guns sticking out of him than a cactus has needles. Still, I swung him up over my shoulder and then spun back toward the truck.

By the time I got there, Svensdottir had already tossed Palmer her service pistol, and Palmer kept busy picking off a few still-curious Grunts while Svensdottir reloaded her assault rifle. Sam laid down his burden, and he gave me a hand with mine.

Seconds later, we were on our way back out of the plaza, Samrat, Palmer, and I keeping watch over our fallen compatriots laid out on the flatbed while the torn tarp flapped behind us like a tattered blue flag. Sam set to work on the downed troopers, seeing if there was anyone he could save. It was a lost cause—but then what part of our impromptu rescue operation hadn't been?

"Thanks," Palmer said from the spot where she'd collapsed. She wiped the blood off her helmet's faceplate. "I owe you one."

"It's on the house," I said. She'd already done Alpha-Nine a huge favor, whether she knew it or not, and her teammates had paid for it with their lives.

SEVEN

I didn't see Sarah Palmer for years after that. Hell, I didn't even think much about her. I was too busy fighting the Covenant War, during which I lost far more friends than I care to think about.

Sam. Gogo. Daughter. All dead long before we finished kicking the Covenant's ass. Maybe that's a story for another day.

By the time the war ended, I was in charge of a new group of ODSTs, although we still called ourselves Alpha-Nine. Humans are funny that way. Case in point: My uncle Lou had a favorite fishing rod he'd haul out during any dull moment. *Had this twenty years,* he'd say with pride as he loaded on a new length of line. *Replaced the rod three times and the reel twice.* I didn't have the heart to tell him there wasn't a single goddamn atom in that rod of his that was there when he originally bought it. But to him, it was the same rod either way, just like the new squad I had was still Alpha-Nine.

Well, at least to High Command.

Of course, on that day back in 2546, Veronica Dare threatened to bring me up on a charge of insubordination. When Alpha-Nine got back to the base, she hauled us all into a conference room—a place as far from the battlefield as possible—and debriefed the entire team at once in the rawest possible terms. I let her go on until she began to run out of ways to describe how irresponsible I was, and then put up a hand to speak. She snarled at me but gave me a go-ahead nod.

"While we might have been on an ONI operation, *you* are not my boss. We were seconded to your command as a courtesy. If you have a problem with my performance, I suggest you take it up with my *actual* superiors."

She gave me a glare hard enough to cut diamonds. "I need to have a word with you in private."

"There's no need for that." I glanced around at the others. Samrat and Gomez were trying not to laugh at me, and Svensdottir just rolled her eyes.

"Go ahead and hash it out with her, Gunny," she said. "The rest of us don't need to listen to it."

Veronica gave her a sharp nod of thanks. "The rest of you are dismissed."

Sam and Gomez almost tripped over each other in their rush to get out of the room. Svensdottir strolled after them, shaking her head.

I shoved back my chair and put my boots up on the conference table in the center of the room. Veronica remained standing and stared down at me with unblinking anger.

"Is this about us?" she said. "Is that why you feel the need to subvert my authority every chance you get?"

I put up my hands. "I wasn't under the impression there was an *us* for this to be about. I mean, you were the one who didn't say a word to me for a year."

She looked away. "Then I guess you're absolutely right."

"Look." I put my feet down and leaned forward on the table. "That may have been one of the greatest weeks of my life—sure, that's a low bar for me, considering I've spent my entire adulthood fighting the Covenant—but my decision to go help Gamma-Six had nothing to do with us. Whatever *us* is."

"It's nothing." She rubbed her forehead. "Nothing at all."

I don't mind telling you how that stabbed me in the heart.

"I understand why you did it," she said. "But you have no idea how much you risked by pulling that stunt. That data chip you rescued has already been paid for with too many good people's blood."

I pulled the chip out of the case in which I'd hidden it and put it down on the table as gently as if it were made of spun glass. I slid it across the smooth surface to her, and she scooped it up without touching my fingers once.

"If we're going to work together, Buck, you need to trust me. There will be things I can't always tell you—things you don't need to know—but you need to believe I have our best interests at heart."

"Our? *Our* who?" I stood up.

"Humanity's."

I pursed my lips at her and nodded. "I believe *you* believe that, but here's my problem. We *do* have a history, and I wouldn't say that it's based on mutual trust."

She looked down at the data chip in her open palm and then closed her hand around it. "You've got that right. Dismissed."

It's hard to believe that we wound up together again after that, I know, but it was a long war. We couldn't duck each other forever—especially not when the stakes were at their highest. She avoided me as long as she could, and I'm not too proud to admit I did the same, right up until the Covenant found and invaded Earth in 2552.

But I'll get to that in a bit. Sorry if I'm jumping around here. That's how I'm hardwired. Try to keep up.

Once the war officially ended and hostilities with the Covenant wound down in 2553, I took the opportunity to put in for some shore leave with Veronica. She'd long since gotten over being furious with me about the Sargasso mission—hell, it had been about seven years—and by then, maybe it was time to see if we might have a future together.

It's almost impossible for a soldier to maintain a relationship during wartime. It's even harder to date an ONI officer at *any* given time. But with the shooting coming to an end, we decided to head to the beaches of the colony of Sundown and give it a shot.

I'll admit I had my doubts. Romances under fire have a tendency to cool down when the pressure's off and you realize you might actually have a tomorrow to live for. It's one thing to blast your way out of New Mombasa together like we did, and an entirely different kind of challenge to plan some kind of future with each other in it.

ODSTs are notoriously bad at thinking about retirement, much less finding someone to spend it with, and I fully expected everything to fall apart within days, if not hours.

On the other hand, if you can't find a good way to woo someone on Sundown, there may not be any hope for you. It's a water world filled with archipelagoes of mountainous islands that stab up from the tropical waves like rows of teeth. Cable cars move you from peak to peak via cable lines that string the islands together like pearls.

The planet has this odd tilt to it that, combined with its

particular sun, lights the sky up like it's sunset for the entire day. The nights are even better, with an aurora borealis that dances sheets of blue, green, and pink lights throughout the brilliant, starry sky. Add the gentle rolling of the surf everywhere you go, and it cannot be beat.

Our luxury tiki hut was one of a series of private villas that stood out on wooden pillars above a long stretch of shallow, sheltered sea. As you walked out on the balcony or along the boardwalks that connected the villas like dots in a kid's activity vid, you could look down and see *cephradons*, giant manta ray–like creatures swooping below you, winging their way between playful crèches of indigenous *navorcas*, curious sea mammals more like dolphins than anything else. We spent a lot of time out there, sipping boat drinks, soaking in the sun, and swimming in the warm, salty water.

We'd been on Sundown a full week, and I'll be damned if we weren't still having the time of our lives. I've known a fair few people in my life, but I never fit with anyone the way I did with Veronica. We even dared to start talking about a life together, like it might actually happen.

Then the big damn combat boot of our careers dropped spikes-first between us.

It began with a knock on the door of our private floating villa—a gentle rap that we tried to ignore, which built into a persistent pounding. I shouted at it to go away.

By the time it came to a crescendo that sounded like a gravity hammer beating on a slab of bedrock, I was ready to fire bullets through the door, but Veronica stopped me with a gentle hand. She had a gun in the other one, sure, but she always has the calmer head.

"Who is it?" she called, as if the intruder hadn't stopped just shy of breaking down the door.

A smooth male voice replied: "My name is Jun, and I'm with the SPARTAN-IV program. I'm here on official business."

I hated those two words. "Official business" always meant a hard day at the office for me.

This was no exception.

I actually glanced out toward the balcony and the open sea beyond. Maybe Veronica and I could make it to the water before this guy got through the door. With a little luck, we might be able to slip free.

I gave her a look and jerked my head toward the balcony. She rolled her eyes at me and waved the door open.

I did my best to mask my disappointment at her decision as Jun strolled into the room. In the warm Sundown air, we were sweating in our swimsuits, but he stood there dressed in black business attire as if he'd just strolled into a climate-controlled boardroom.

I'd met him before, on Reach, just before it fell back in 2552, but we'd both been armored up—me as an ODST and him as a Spartan. I'd never seen his face, which featured a tattoo on his left cheek of a fist holding three arrows.

Like every Spartan, he towered over us, nearly scraping his bald head on the top of the doorway. He carried himself with a quiet power that reminded you he could kill everyone within sight in a matter of seconds. You lived only because he had no reason to destroy you.

"I apologize for disturbing you during your leave."

I grimaced and made way for him to enter the main room. "No one's sorrier than me."

He found a seat on one of the embroidered blue pillows that lay scattered about the place, and he smiled up at me. "I didn't say I was sorry."

I opened my mouth to propose a number of ways I could remedy that particular problem for him. To her credit, Veronica recognized that was coming and spoke up first. "Exactly why are you here?"

"To speak to Sergeant Buck."

That set me back. I'd assumed he was there for Veronica, and I didn't care for his gaze to turn toward me. I eyed the balcony again, but leaned back against the door to the villa's bedroom and folded my arms across my chest instead. "Okay. So speak."

"Privately." He glanced at Veronica, and now it was her turn to be taken aback. It was one thing to not be the subject of the conversation, but an ONI official being kicked out of the room jet-jumped right over that.

"Her clearance level is far higher than mine," I said.

"Not for this."

I pushed off the wall and took a step toward him. "I'm telling you, anything you can say to me, you can say in front of her."

Veronica put a hand on my chest. "Just forget it." She ducked past me and grabbed a sundress, then slipped it on over her head as she made for the door.

I glared at Jun. "I'm just going to tell her, anyway."

She spun on me from the open doorway. "No, you're not."

I tried to protest, but she cut me off.

"I'm ONI, Eddie. I know the rules."

"But—"

"There are lots of things I can't tell you. It's only fair you have some of your own."

She zipped out the door before I could say another word. I considered going after her, but between her and the Spartan, I didn't see how that could go well. I turned back to Jun.

"It appears you now have my undivided attention."

"I'll try to be brief." Jun resettled himself to face me. "You're familiar with the Spartans."

"I've encountered my fair share."

He gave me a nod of acknowledgment. "You served with the 11th Shock Troops Battalion on Reach."

"That I did. Spartan-B312 helped me out of a pinch in New Alexandria."

Jun bowed his head. "Noble Six was a good man."

I gave him a moment to collect himself. He still had eyes as dry as a glassed desert.

"You have an exemplary combat record, Sergeant Buck. You're a fantastic leader. One of the finest soldiers in the ODST."

"You're making me blush."

"Just because the Covenant War is over doesn't mean there aren't battles to be fought."

"Is this some kind of recruiting drive? Because I still have a good while left on my current tour."

"Recruiting? In a way." He sized me up. "How would you like to become a Spartan?"

That caught me so off guard I actually laughed out loud.

"It's not a joke," Jun said.

"Of course it's not." I tried to maintain my composure. "But aren't I a little old for that? Unless ONI's recovered some kind of Covenant youth ray?"

Jun stood up. He didn't crack even the slightest smile. "We're in the process of launching a new program. The Spartan-IVs. We'd like you to be a member of our first class of recruits."

That stopped me like a pair of underwear made of ice. "Wait. You're serious."

"Always."

It takes a lot to make me speechless, but he'd rung my bell hard. "How . . . ?"

"Building on the SPARTAN-II and SPARTAN-III programs,

we've developed a means of improving existing soldiers to super-human levels of strength, speed, durability, and endurance. This isn't something that could have been efficiently accomplished in earlier years, but with advances over the course of the war, it's finally attainable."

"And then you don't have to take children from their families anymore either."

Now that got his attention. By this point, I was pretty much convinced of the rumors I'd heard, about how ONI had kidnapped children from their homes to induct them into the SPARTAN program, but no one I'd talked with had ever been able to back that up. The way the mention of it tweaked Jun's nose out of joint gave me the first real confirmation that the horrible tales had to be true.

Despite that, Jun remained a professional. He recomposed his features and gestured at himself. "I was actually an orphan myself, but yes, that's an excellent side effect."

I slumped against the wall behind me and rubbed the stubble on my chin that Veronica didn't seem to mind. I didn't know how she'd feel about me becoming some kind of super-soldier, though, and was reluctant to ask.

"What about the rest of my team?" I asked.

Jun shook his head. "This is a highly selective program. We're only looking for the best."

That got my hackles up. "They *are* the best. I'd have been buried a dozen times over without them."

"We have your combat records, Sergeant. Not just your reports, but the full set of data your armor collects, plus an AI dedicated to analyzing them. We know full well who's been saving whom."

"Seems like an awful lot of trouble to go to for little old me."

"You're not the only one I'm having this conversation with. Just one of the few."

"And the others don't include anyone else from Alpha-Nine."

"No disrespect intended. They're good soldiers, Sergeant, every one of them. Even that one you call the Rookie. But speaking to that point, none of them have your skills or experience."

"They're learning faster than I ever did."

"That's not true."

"And I suppose your AI can prove it."

Jun nodded.

I narrowed my eyes at the man. He wasn't going to give me anything on this, and I knew it. Spartans don't bargain much, and even if he wanted to, I sensed he didn't have the authority. He wasn't making the rules here, just carrying them out.

"How much time do I have?"

Jun gestured toward the door. "I have a shuttle waiting for us. We can leave right now."

"I meant, to decide."

That surprised him. "Ah. Not much. Our first class is already well under way. I would have come to recruit you sooner, but Commander Musa decided to let you enjoy your leave."

"My leave's not over until tomorrow."

"We didn't want you to waste too much time making any new plans."

I didn't know if that was a thinly veiled reference to my advancing relationship with Veronica or not. I didn't really care.

"Will there be a second class?"

"Maybe. A lot depends on the quality of soldiers we can induct into the first class. Programs have to prove themselves to survive."

I'll admit it. I thought about it. I actually considered it.

I mean, wouldn't you? As much as I didn't care for the Spartans as an idea, every one of them I'd ever met had been a solid person.

They weren't the most sociable types, but they got the job—*any* job—done. You could trust any one of them with your life.

But I already had a team that trusted me with their lives, and I couldn't just abandon them like that.

I gotta admit, though, the idea of being transformed into a world-saving super-soldier with the power to drive your foes before you had its allure. I was mighty tempted.

I looked toward the door Veronica had disappeared through. We'd only just started thinking about our lives together. What would becoming something more than human do to that?

"Thanks," I said, "but I'm going to have to say no."

Jun looked as stunned as if I'd spat on his best outfit, then said: "You do realize the opportunity you're turning down here, Sergeant?"

"The chance to become the kind of superhero every kid dreams about. Yeah. I've seen the marketing vids."

"I hope this isn't some kind of negotiating tactic. The answer about the rest of your team is final."

"As is mine."

Jun shook his head in disbelief and moved toward the door. "All right, then. It's your choice," he said. "We don't want anyone in the program who isn't committed one hundred percent."

"Which is why my answer has to be no."

He grunted at that. "They told me you'd be straight with me."

"Haven't I been?"

"Like a laser."

He was about to leave when I shot him one more question. "How many others have turned you down?"

"You mean, how many dedicated UNSC soldiers have declined the opportunity to become part of the next wave of super-soldiers capable of securing peace throughout the galaxy?" Jun shrugged. "Take a guess."

"I don't think I could."

"None, Sergeant," he said flatly. "You're the first."

A dagger pierced my belly. "My mother always said I was special."

"Well, she got that right, I suppose. She just didn't know how."

"She also mentioned 'especially stubborn' from time to time."

"May she rest in peace." Jun stopped himself, then stuck out his hand, and I shook it. "It's been an honor. Please extend my apologies to Captain Dare for my quick departure."

"You have a galaxy to go save. I'll get back to doing the same. In my own way. Tomorrow though."

When he was gone, I wandered over to the bar in the villa's main room and poured myself a stiff drink. Then I went out onto the balcony to enjoy the dying rays of the last sunset of my leave, giving thanks that I'd never have to explain the situation to Veronica. She wouldn't even ask what the Spartan and I talked about, but a part of me wondered if she knew already just the same.

EIGHT

Come to the truth of it, I almost said yes to Jun that day on Sundown, but the idea that I'd have to abandon my teammates—and maybe Veronica, too—just galled me. I'd been through hell with the latest version of Alpha-Nine, and like my uncle Lou and his fishing rod, I couldn't bear to part with it.

I understood how the others Jun recruited had all said yes. It was the opportunity of a lifetime, and it held the potential for being able to do a whole lot more good for humanity. But it struck me as a bargain with the devil. You could have everything you wanted. It would only cost you your soul.

I'd seen too many members of Alpha-Nine give everything they had—up to and including their lives. I had fought alongside Dutch, Mickey, and Romeo for so long at this point, leaving them behind would have made me feel like a traitor. If anything ever happened to any of them in the field from that time forward, I knew I'd blame myself forever for not being there to save them.

Maybe because of that, we stopped adding people to Alpha-Nine when the war ended. The Rookie turned out to be our final recruit. He filled up the open spot created after Gramps died in August of 2552, during the battle for Reach.

Baruti Komen—or Gramps, as we called him—had been the sole survivor of his previous unit, and High Command had matched him with Alpha-Nine to fill yet another hole in our ranks that had opened up in early '52. Gramps had joined the UNSC the moment the Covenant invaded human space, which meant he'd served even longer than me. I outranked him, but he always claimed that was only because he'd spent so much more time in cryosleep, heading off to more important skirmishes.

"That's the secret to my success," I said. "I don't sleep so much on the job."

He laughed pretty hard at that.

Gramps wasn't with us all that long. He took a burst of plasma in the chest during the fall of Reach. Blew out his heart. We've got a lot of amazing medical technology these days, but nothing that can help with a wound like that.

We hadn't been doing anything particularly special or desperate at the time—just trying to hold a piece of ground on one patch of dirt on Reach for some reason only High Command understood and wasn't particularly eager to share with us. Some days, you're the feint, and other days you're the actual attack. You just don't always get told which kind of day it might be.

I don't know if Gramps died for some noble cause or to pave the way for someone else's noble cause, but either way, we couldn't save him.

After Reach fell to the Covenant, we hauled ass back home to help out with the Battle for Earth. And on the way, High Command saddled us with the Rookie. Maybe it's not fair that we never called him anything else, but that's what he was to us: a brand-spanking-new trooper who'd been transferred to our squad at the last possible second.

Never mind that he was a seasoned veteran who had five years on Mickey. He was the last new person our fireteam ever saw. Maybe if someone else had joined up, we'd have gotten around to giving the Rookie a better name. But that never happened.

When we got to Earth, the Covenant had already set up shop over Kenya. But instead of just glassing the homefront—as we'd feared for decades that they might do the instant they found our ancestral homeworld—they'd gone hunting for something in New Mombasa. The High Command decided to take advantage of that odd lull in the impending armageddon by hitting the bastards as hard as we could.

Alpha-Nine—along with the rest of us Helljumpers present on the UNSC *Say My Name*—had orders to drop straight on top of the Covenant assault carrier *Solemn Penance*, which sat hovering right over the city. Our job was to board the damn thing, fight our way through to the bridge, and yank it out of the hands of a Covenant leader known as the Prophet of Regret.

We hoped to help him live up to his name, maybe even nab the bastard to broker a peace deal—if such a thing was possible.

But Veronica intercepted us before we could climb into our coffins. I cringed when she walked in. Whatever she wanted, I figured it couldn't be good.

After all, it had to be important enough that she'd track me down personally in the middle of the Battle for Earth. On top of that, remember that I hadn't seen her for a whole six years after that mission on Sargasso, and we'd finished that on pretty lousy terms.

Sure, it would all work out soon afterward, but I had no hopes for that in the moment. When she grabbed me, I just knew her timing was lousy.

Under Veronica's orders—or maybe from someone else a level way above my pay grade—Alpha-Nine got seconded to ONI for another mission under her command. She refused to tell us anything about this new job—only that we were to follow her orders to the letter. My relationships didn't normally deteriorate in that direction, but I'd done enough work with ONI over the years. I knew how to dance to that beat.

She didn't do much to alter our original plan until after we'd launched from our dropship. At that point, she gave us new coordinates to head for, steering us away from *Solemn Penance* and putting us straight into the streets of New Mombasa instead.

I actually considered ignoring her and leading Alpha-Nine to crash-land into the Covenant flagship per our original orders. But I was a good soldier that day, and it ended up saving our lives.

Right after we switched our target, *Solemn Penance* triggered a jump into slipspace while it was still in the Earth's atmosphere. This is what we call a Very Bad Thing.

The shock wave from that insane activation blew out an electromagnetic pulse bigger than a conventional nuke's. It fried the electronics of just about everything around it—and that included every one of the midair drop pods carrying a Helljumper.

Alpha-Nine was the only team to survive, and that was a damn narrow thing at best. If we hadn't veered off under Veronica's orders, we'd have hurtled to our deaths in those blacked-out coffins along with everyone else. That's the one thing every ODST with any bit of sanity left in them wakes up screaming in fear of at one point or another, and it kills me to think about how many good soldiers met their ends that way on that day.

As it was, each one of us had a hard landing. The shock wave not only blacked out our systems but knocked Alpha-Nine all over the place. Instead of hitting our target like a sniper's bullet, we wound up landing more like bits of buckshot.

Mickey and the Rookie actually smacked into each other on the way down. I figured both of them for dead, but they turned out to be tougher than I could have hoped.

I landed upside down, which made getting out of my pod

trickier than ever. I managed to get Veronica on the comm in her drop pod, but I couldn't raise anyone else. That worried me, but I consoled myself with the fact that I at least still had her on the line.

ONI must make their coffins out of tougher stuff, but Veronica had gotten stuck inside hers and couldn't get the door open. That meant I had to come to her, someplace in Tayari Plaza.

The mean and shattered streets of New Mombasa were swarming with Covenant forces, though, and it took me too damn long to cut my way through them. At the time, I thought it strange that I didn't see any Elites swarming over the place. There had been plenty on Reach, after all.

Turns out the Covenant was having internal problems at the time. The Brutes and the Elites didn't care much for each other to begin with, and as it happened, they were about to thrash out their differences for good. They later called it the Great Schism, although at the time it just seemed like the Giant Fustercluck.

Apparently the Prophet of Regret had jumped the gun and taken his fleet to attack Earth before the Prophet of Truth was ready to roll. (Please don't ask me how many prophets the Covenant had. Even one of them was too damn many for me.)

Right after Regret jumped out of Earth's atmosphere, Truth gave the orders to get to it. He had a planet or two's worth of Brutes loyal to him embedded in Regret's fleet. They slaughtered any Elites that had been left behind and then set in to treating any humans they found the same way. I hear most of the Covenant—particularly the Elites—weren't privy to this sudden change of plans until weeks later, but by then, it was too late for them to do anything about it.

Et tu, Brute, anyone?

While I was happy to not have to face off against any Elites—

they earned every letter of that nickname—I wasn't sure I would have traded them for ten times as many Brutes on the ground.

But they never ask me for my opinion about these things, you know.

It was late in the day when I crashed into New Mombasa, and it was getting dark fast. The local cops had done their best to protect the citizens from the invasion, but what police department is prepped to repel a full-scale alien assault?

Alone as I was, and not knowing if any of my teammates were alive, I tried to keep to the shadows when and where I could. Much as I enjoyed killing the bugs that had finally dared to invade Earth, that wasn't my mission.

The frustrating part was that Veronica hadn't yet briefed me on what the hell Alpha-Nine's mission actually was, and I had to rescue her before I could figure that out.

The Covenant forces flooding the city made that a challenge. Although I didn't know it at the time, they had a mission of their own beyond just killing every human they could see, which they could have done from orbit. They were hunting for something they'd detected underneath the city, and they wanted it badly.

Despite their huge numbers, that forced the Covenant to spread themselves thin, which gave me a fighting chance. I avoided them as best I could, but sometimes they just popped up in places I *had* to go through. When that happened, I disposed of them as fast as I could and then moved on before anyone could come looking to see what all the excitement was about.

I'd almost made it to Veronica's location when she reported enemy forces moving in on her position. I made a mad dash to get there in time to save her, but a stubborn pair of Hunters spoiled my plans.

Have you ever seen one of those beasts? Believe it or not, they're not actually single creatures at all. They're colonies of space worms banded together in the shape of giants. Angry, slimy giants with nearly impenetrable armor and massive guns.

Better yet, they twin up, which means they always come in pairs.

If you ever have the misfortune to meet a pair of these monsters on a darkened street in New Mombasa while a battle for the future of your species rages around you, run the hell away. If that's not an option for you—and it sure wasn't for me—run circles around the lumbering bastards and shoot them in the back.

I don't normally advocate for cheap shots like that, but hey, it's war. And, two, they carry these enormous shields on their forearms that repel bullets like they were spitwads. Shoot them anywhere but there.

But the back is easiest.

By the time I took care of those giant freaks, I'd already lost contact with Veronica. I finally reached her pod in a panic and tore the door off it, thinking I'd find her either grateful or dead.

To my utter shock, her coffin stood empty.

I was so distracted by this discovery that I didn't see an Engineer coming around the back of the pod at me, carrying Veronica's helmet. I'd never seen one of the floaters up close before, and I'm only a little ashamed to admit that I panicked.

I stumbled over backward trying to get away from it. I thought it was going to try to beat me to death with Veronica's headgear, just to put a nail in my absolute failure to rescue her.

That's when Romeo put a high-caliber bullet through that gasbag, firing from the top of a building across the plaza. The thing didn't just deflate; it exploded hard enough to embed Veronica's helmet in a nearby wall. I didn't see where it went, but the Rookie pried it out of there later while he was hunting for the rest of us.

Grateful as I was for the save, I had some mixed feelings about that.

Romeo and I rendezvoused as soon as we could. I wasn't posi-tive Veronica was dead—along with maybe Mickey, Dutch, or the Rookie—but I had no idea where she might be and no way to find her. Since she hadn't disclosed anything about the mission, I couldn't follow up on that piece of business either.

With the city overrun by heavily armed Covenant forces, one thing seemed clear. It was time for Romeo and me to get the hell out of town before it became a sheet of glass.

We didn't know it at the time, but every member of Alpha-Nine had survived, too. Dutch landed in the Uplift Nature Re-serve and had to commandeer a Warthog and use it to shoot his way onto the island proper. He wound up stumbling over Mickey, who'd commandeered a Scorpion tank himself and was using it to blast his way across the city.

I never accused my teammates of being subtle.

While Romeo and I were still looking for them, Dutch and Mickey got drafted into helping ONI defend Alpha Site, their headquarters in New Mombasa, until they could get charges in place to destroy it. ONI was afraid the Covenant would be able to use the collected intelligence gathered inside the building against humanity, but the officers and analysts there didn't seem to know a damn thing about high explosives.

Dutch and Mickey were only too happy to help them out. I never knew those guys to give up the chance to make things go boom in the service of the UNSC—especially if some of those things were useful to the Covenant.

The Alpha Site was this massive black cube of a building, walled and moated off on the southernmost edge of New Mombasa, and the only way to get to it on foot was over a bridge that connected the joint to the rest of the island. Dutch and Mickey blew the bridge, which slowed down the Covenant advance on their location, but that was all. It didn't stop the Covenant soldiers from piling into their Phantoms and dropping in from above.

That at least meant that the Covenant had to stuff its assault teams into convenient, ship-sized packages, which made for great target practice, but those Phantoms are damn sturdy. The guns ONI had on hand couldn't do much to bring them down. Instead, Dutch and Mickey led the troops there in a retreating action, doing their best to slow the assault long enough for the local cops to set charges inside the building. The plan was to bring the whole site down and seal off the top-secret stuff buried deep below it.

Once those were in place, Dutch and Mickey wound up falling all the way back to Alpha Site's rooftop and then hopping on the last Pelican out of there, abandoning the entire place to the enemy— but not for long. When they got clear, Mickey triggered the charges lining the building's interior and blasted the whole thing to hell.

After that, Dutch and Mickey finally got close enough that our comms started working again. I can't tell you how thrilled I was to hear their voices. Romeo had spent most of the day trying to convince me to give up hope on them, and rubbing his face in all of his dire predictions made their survival that much sweeter.

It also meant there was hope that Veronica might be alive, too.

After the mission on Sargasso, I'd buried any feelings I had for her as deep as I could go. Seeing her again had dredged a lot of them up, but in an angry, frustrated way. The thought that she might still be breathing filled me with such hope—I realized that I hadn't done nearly as good a job of getting over her as I'd thought.

Romeo and I had headed over to the New Mombasa Police Department's headquarters to do what we could to lend a hand— and maybe find a way out of town. I ordered Dutch and Mickey to rendezvous with us there, and Romeo and I double-timed it up to the roof to meet them.

The city's police had given up on trying to fight the Covenant. They didn't have the numbers or the guns. Instead, they were doing everything they could to evacuate the city as fast as possible.

I have to give them credit for how well they dealt with the panic. Lots of police officers, when faced with the invasion of their planet, run home to take care of their families first. But these people considered the rest of their city to be their family, and they did their absolute best to help them.

It wasn't enough, of course, but what could be? We'd all assumed the Covenant would just start glassing Earth as soon as they arrived.

Despite the efforts, though, lots of people did horrible things to each other as they tried to flee the city. Fights broke out. Innocents got trampled . . . children, even.

By the time we got there, most of the screaming and terror was already over. Alpha-Nine had only the growing horror of relative silence punctuated by the sounds of plasma fire, burning buildings, and orders being barked out by Brute commanders.

In less than a day, the city had gone from being one of the most vibrant places on Earth to an alien-riddled ghost town. I figured it was time for us to be leaving, too.

When I saw Dutch and Mickey's Pelican heading in to land on the NMPD's rooftop helipad, I thought, *That's just what we were going to do.* Romeo and I would join the other guys, and we'd beat a trail out of there, leaving nothing but our dust behind.

But just when they were touching down and we were about to have ourselves a family reunion, a pair of Banshees swooped in and knocked the Pelican clear off the landing pad. It went scudding sideways through the sky and landed in a fiery wreck on another rooftop across the way.

Those two Banshees turned out to be the sharp end of an

assault against the few cops that remained alive. Seems the Covenant had pegged us as one of the last bastions of humanity in the city, and they meant to put a bloody end to that.

As plasma fire rained down on us, I grabbed Romeo, and we raced over to see what we could do for our downed friends. Unfortunately, they'd crashed on a completely separate building. There just wasn't any easy way to get to where we needed to be.

In the end, Romeo and I had to tiptoe across a bundle of girders dangling from a crane to reach the rooftop where the Pelican had come to rest. The pilot was dead, and the bird was a total loss anyway, but some NMPD cops had rallied around Dutch and Mickey to give them fireteam support until we arrived.

By the time Romeo and I got there, it seemed like every flying alien within a hundred klicks had been drawn to the Pelican's wreckage like moths to a bonfire. If they were looking for light, well, we made it bright enough to burn them all out of the sky.

Then the Phantoms arrived. They dropped off their troops by the shipload and kept coming back with more in wave after goddamn wave.

The top of that building ran thick with Covenant blood.

It was a long, miserable fight, more of a test of our endurance than our skill. When you're in a target-rich environment like that, it's hard to miss. You just have to keep fighting until you get the chance to be a little choosier.

Right about when I thought we'd seen the last of them and might find ourselves some breathing room, this Brute chieftain came leaping down out of the last enemy transport. He was swinging this gigantic gravity hammer, raining hell down on our heads. He took out a cop with a single blow, then turned around and smashed down Romeo, too.

Once Romes was flat on his back, the chieftain spun the gravity hammer's shaft in his hands, bringing the bladed side of its business end to bear. Then he slammed it down into Romeo's shoulder. That damn thing hit so hard it snapped Romeo's sniper rifle in half and went right through his armor.

Going for the kill, the chieftain brought his hammer back over his head, intending for a two-handed chop with every bit of his weight behind it. Just as he was about to give dozens of ladies across the galaxy a reason to weep over Romeo, I saw my opening and jumped on the Brute's back. I brought my knife down into that monster's neck over and over, but he didn't seem any more annoyed about it than if I'd been one of those bat-shaped leeches that used to feed on the octowhales back home.

Mickey got in on the fun and tackled the chieftain, too. He managed to hold the thing still long enough for Dutch to charge the Brute like a bullet train and knock him flat. The humongous beast landed on my knife, and simple physics drove my blade into him better than I ever could. I was so dedicated to killing the Covenant bastard, though, that I couldn't get out of the way as he fell. He landed square on top of me, and it took both Mickey and Dutch to haul his carcass off.

Turned out Romeo was a lot worse. The chieftain's gravity hammer had bitten deep into his chest, and the way he was wheezing, I knew he'd punctured a lung. We needed to get him medical attention fast, but with the Pelican down, our ride was gone, so we had to leg it out of there instead.

I didn't see any percentage in trying to walk through the streets, though, as the Covenant completely owned New Mombasa by that point. So I slung one of Romeo's arms over my shoulders and headed for the nearest train stop: Kikowani Station. I figured from there we could slip into one of the maglev tunnels and haul ass right out of town under the Covenant's noses. We hustled down that way, stopping only long enough for me to use a can of biomedical foam to seal up Romeo's punctured lung.

It was dark when we reached the station, and the first thing we discovered was that the Covenant had breached the nearby seawalls, and the tunnels had been flooded. We weren't getting out that way.

The med foam had Romeo back on his feet again, but even if he'd been at a hundred percent, we had zero chance of fighting our way out of the city. Not before the Covenant finally got tired of hunting around for whatever they were looking for and just glassed the whole place.

But there's a reason I'm in charge of Alpha-Nine. 'Cause I never give up, goddammit. Call me the man with the plan.

Just when the others seemed about to lose hope, I spotted the glowing lights of a Phantom skimming low overhead, and I pointed up at our last shot at getting out of there. "We're going to steal that ride. It's landing. Now's our chance!"

I grabbed Mickey, and we headed for the Phantom, leaving Dutch to watch over Romeo. The entire time we raced over to it, I'll admit I was terrified. What if the ship didn't land? Or took off before we reached it?

When Mickey and I got there, it wasn't as bad as I'd feared, but that's only because I can fear it up pretty good. The transport was in the process of dropping off a payload of Covenant troops and we lit them up.

Just as I thought we were making some headway, another Phantom joined the first for a moment and dropped off some fresh fodder to join the fight.

We had to move fast before that happened again, or we'd wind up batting an unending flow of garbage. We killed everything in sight before that second Phantom came back for more. And then the Covies came streaming up at us out of the darkness anyhow. It was like they'd been entrenched there forever and *we* were the invaders.

While I kept the ground troops busy, Mickey made his way into the Phantom and took over the ship. Thankfully, between training sims and just raw intuition, he was able to pilot the hell out of that thing.

While he zoomed back for Dutch and Romeo, I hijacked myself a Banshee. Believe it or not, because the Covenant was spending so much time trying to root humans out of the city's buildings, they'd left plenty of their one-man combat flyers lying around, just waiting for me to steal them.

I mean, how convenient!

I quickly caught up with the Phantom. I would have loved to be able to just jump into that big boat with the rest of my team and take off into the sky, but the Covenant still ruled the higher altitudes. We kept low to the ground instead. We caught a lot of fire that way, but it beat being shot down by something much bigger.

The worst part of it for me came the few times the way through was blocked. I had to actually get out of my stolen Banshee and fight forward far enough on foot that I could clear the way for the Phantom. I could have ordered one of the others to do it, but Romeo was hurt, Mickey was the only one who had a prayer of flying the Phantom in a straight line, and Dutch—let's just say I didn't have the heart to make him do something I wasn't ready to do myself.

I had many chances to regret adopting that strategy. The biggest one came when we had to face off against the Covenant's greatest ground weapon: the Scarab. It's a tank the size of a building that walks around on four legs bent like a spider's, and it bristles with enough weaponry to qualify as a mobile demolition platform.

Pro tip: Shoot them in the legs first. And it's okay to cheer when you blow one of them up. You deserve it.

That whole march out of the occupied parts of New Mombasa might have felt a lot like victory if it hadn't been for the fact that the Covenant had already won. We were just trying to find a way to be gone. But dammit if we didn't make it.

It wasn't until I rejoined the rest of the team on the Phantom that I realized that I'd made a mistake.

I checked in on Romeo to see how he was doing. He grinned up at me and said, "Just glad we didn't go with your first plan. Look at those tunnels. Ones that aren't flooded are probably packed with buggers. Hell, I wouldn't go down there even if you ordered me to."

And that's when I knew where Veronica had gone on her mission.

One of the Covenant species is called the Yanme'e, although we usually refer to them as Drones or buggers. They're these flying creatures that swarm over the places they're sent, and they come at you like a bunch of angry hornets. I sometimes think of them as trolls because they like to hide under things like bridges and then ambush you at the worst possible moments.

They're built kinda like beetles, and they flit around on twinned pairs of transparent wings that flap faster than you can see. They get enough lift out of them—and some strange Covie tech—that they can pick up a fully armored trooper with these vicious claws on the ends of their feet and haul him into the sky. Once that happens, you're in bad shape for sure.

The first thing the Drones usually do when they set up in a place is build a hive made of spit, shit, and whatever else they can find lying around. It's how they mark a conquered area as their own.

Despite their hive mentality—or maybe because of it—the

buggers are just as sentient as any other Covenant species. And because it's hard to hide behind cover from someone who can just fly over it, I find them even more dangerous. They're not all that great in tight quarters or for carrying heavy weapons, but in the right place and time, they're deadly foes.

If the Drones were infesting the tunnels under New Mombasa, it had to be because the Covenant had sent them there to conquer that space. But why would they do that? We don't keep our soldiers underground, so there's not much down there for them to go after.

Unless they were sent in after something else. A nonmilitary target that had some kind of value to the Covenant. Enough to pull the Drones away from the open-sky battlefield and shove them under New Mombasa to look for it.

My money was on ONI being smart enough to realize this. And if so, that meant they'd sent Veronica there to defend or recover whatever the Drones were after. She'd then come to Alpha-Nine for support, and so far, we hadn't done a very good job of providing that.

I knew the guys weren't going to like it. I mean, we'd just escaped the worst battle our planet had ever seen. But I made the command decision to go back and see if we could complete Veronica's mission, the one thing that had been so important she'd pulled us away from raiding the Prophet of Regret's flagship and trying to save Earth. Whatever she'd been after, if it was that vital to the UNSC, I couldn't bring myself to ignore it.

And, to be honest, some small part of me hoped to hell we might find her, too.

Under the cover of night, I had Mickey fly us back toward the rubble he and Dutch had left behind after they'd blown the hell out of ONI's Alpha Site. The entire city was still swarming with the Covenant, including a couple of Covenant capital ships hovering over the crater the Prophet of Regret had left behind when he shunted his own ship into slipspace.

It turned out that the Covenant was actually hunting all over the city for a portal to the Ark, a Forerunner installation from which they could fire all of the Halo rings across the galaxy at once. This was put in place to destroy the Flood and keep those monsters from wiping out the galaxy—by killing all sentient life first.

I know. Forerunner logic doesn't always make much sense.

If you think they were crazy, though, they had nothing on the Covenant, which is based around a religion that *worships* the Forerunners. They thought that firing the Halo rings would launch their so-called "Great Journey," which would uplift the Covenant faithful to the next plane of existence.

Imagine their surprise if they'd actually managed to pull that off. Makes me smile every time.

That didn't concern us at the moment though. I had Mickey keep well clear of the crater. Now that we weren't trying to escape, the other Covenant ships in the area didn't pay much attention to us, but diving into that crater for a closer look would have been painting a "Shoot me!" sign on our backs.

Still, we needed to find some way to get into those tunnels that ran under Alpha Site, the ones that were buried deepest. I didn't know how we'd manage it, but I knew that we'd find whatever Veronica had been after down there.

I had Mickey slow up while we looked for a place to land. "Fly like you belong here," I told him.

As we got closer to the spot where we were supposed to have landed in New Mombasa in the first place, I clapped Mickey on the back and stabbed my finger toward a clear spot. He took my meaning, and the Phantom veered right for it.

I had Mickey drop me off there so I could get a better look, and then I waved him and the others back into the air with orders to head for the shipyards down the Waterfront Highway. That was the only place I could think of that they'd be able to hide for any length of time without making themselves a target.

With the team safe, I slipped through the city under the cover of night until I discovered that—like anywhere else I wanted to get to in that city—the Covenant had beat me to it.

I almost gave up hope and called for Mickey to pick me up and get us the hell out of there. It was one thing to try to finish a mission that we didn't know much about. Call that foolhardy. But diving into certain death? That's just stupid.

That's when I heard Veronica's voice calling for me over the comm. "Buck!"

I can't remember ever being so relieved in my life. I'd just hauled my entire team back into an about-to-be-glassed city on little more than a hunch. Veronica had always stirred strong feelings in me, but I hadn't till that point been a hundred percent sure I could trust them. Hearing her voice meant I'd made the right choice.

It also meant we still had a massive job to do, as soon as we figured out what it was.

"Where the hell are you?" I said.

"Data center, but we're coming out."

"We?"

"No time to explain," Veronica said, "but do not, I repeat, *do not* shoot anything pink!"

I didn't understand at the time, but I found out later that she'd gone into the data center to gather all the data from the Superintendent, this AI that ran every bit of New Mombasa's infrastructure. It sat deep enough below Alpha Site that even Dutch and Mickey's efforts to blow the place to pieces hadn't reached it.

Maybe that was an error on their part, or maybe that had been by ONI design. It's hard to tell with those spooks. Either way, I was thrilled to find out it meant that they hadn't killed Veronica by accident.

And the cherry on the top of all that, as an unbelievable bonus, was that Veronica had stumbled across the Rookie on her way.

He'd been knocked cold for six hours after his landing and spent the rest of the time playing detective in the middle of a war zone. Trying to track us down had led him to Veronica instead, and he'd joined her on the mission she hadn't yet revealed to the rest of us.

But finding the Rookie still alive and shooting wasn't the biggest surprise that Veronica brought to the surface with her. She had a Huragok with her, too.

The Engineer didn't look all that pink to me. Sure, it's got some pink tips on some of its tentacles, but they're mostly as blue and purplish as a bruised octowhale. So it's a damn good thing I spotted Veronica and the Rookie with him when I found them in the building, or I might have shot him dead.

Turns out that an Engineer isn't a natural thing. When you see one of those gasbags floating over you and reaching out with its purple tentacles and flailing its glowing blue cilia at you, well, that's hard to believe, I know, but work with me here.

The Forerunners who built the Halos—those hoop-shaped artificial worlds with the ability to destroy the entire galaxy?—they also created the Engineers. I don't exactly understand how the Huragok work—no surprise there—but they can fix just about anything you can break. They can also hook up to just about any kind of computer hardware in the galaxy. Forerunner, Covenant, and even human.

The Superintendent wasn't doing so well. I don't know if that had to do with the Covenant attacking the city, the Prophet of Regret entering slipspace right overhead, or the way Mickey and Dutch blew Alpha Site into bite-sized bits, but its data was as corrupt as any politician.

The Engineer though? The smelly bastard tried to fix it. He actually broke away from his Covenant handlers, locked himself in a room with the AI, and gave it a go.

Turns out even advanced biological constructs with computer interfaces at the business ends of their tentacles can't fix everything without the right parts. They can, however, copy data at something like lightspeed, and they have enough onboard storage built into them to keep a full-on AI stuffed in a hip pocket.

If they had pockets. Or wore clothes.

You know what I mean.

While the Engineers had been brought into the Covenant, they hadn't gone willingly. The Covenant had fitted them each with explosive vests and made it clear that if the Engineers didn't follow their orders, they would find themselves transformed into unfixable messes.

That's why other Engineers had been working against us—along with the rest of the Covenant—since we'd arrived. They didn't have any choice.

It's also why they made a large boom after you shot them. It wasn't just their lighter-than-air innards that went up, but those tricky damn vests they'd been welded into.

I gotta admit, when I found out about that, I felt bad for punching the tickets of the few that I'd run across before I met Vergil. But it's not like I could have given them a hug instead.

Some of Vergil's friends had given their lives to get his vest off of him so he could come over to our side to help. They knew the only shot their species had at winning their freedom was ensuring humanity defeated the Covenant, and they were willing to sacrifice themselves for it.

If that's not heroism, then I don't know what is.

To his credit, Vergil made the most of the chance he'd been given. Now it was just up to us to make sure that his pals hadn't given theirs all for nothing.

First thing Veronica did when we had a spare moment was wait until I took off my helmet so she could sock me in the jaw for "abandoning the mission"—the one she hadn't even told me about.

She made up for it a second later by planting on me the kind of kiss that makes a man forget all about who was right and who was wrong. Seems putting me in mortal danger had helped her put her feelings for me in perspective, too. Funny how an alien invasion can do that for you.

Once we got out of the data center and saw how screwed the entire city was, that stripped the warm glow right out of both Veronica and me faster than a dip in the Arctic. We had to fight our way out until we made it to the Waterfront Highway, the main drag out of New Mombasa. By no small coincidence, it also ran straight by the shipyards where the other guys were hiding out in our stolen Phantom. I considered calling them in for a pickup, but the Covenant activity in the air had only grown thicker. Getting them shot down wouldn't be doing any of us any favors.

On the other hand, I didn't see how we were going to be able to escort Vergil all the way down the highway without him getting taken out as well. The only advice I had for Veronica and the Rookie was to make sure we weren't standing too close to him if that happened. At the time, we thought the gas that kept a Huragok floating made for a damn fine explosive on its own—whether he was wearing a vest or not—and could go off if he got punctured.

But I'll be damned if that Engineer didn't crawl inside a nearby garbage truck and get it up and running again. Veronica jumped in the driver's seat and took off for the shipyards, daring me to keep up.

I'll say this for her: She never failed to impress me with her bravery and her willingness to do whatever it took to get the mission done. Much as her dedication to the job frustrated me at times, I loved that about her, too.

As I told the Rookie then, *If you ever fall for a woman, make sure she's got balls.*

Ah, hell, you know what I mean.

Words to live by.

The Rookie and I scared up an abandoned Warthog and chased after Veronica and Vergil's truck. We caught up with them fast and escorted them out of the city. But the Covenant hadn't exactly forgotten about the highways—maybe because they were worried about an assault coming *into* the city. Either way, the garbage truck made a poor excuse for a tank, and escorting the thing out of town made for a crappy Sunday drive.

First chance we got, we swapped the Warthog for a Scorpion and put the tank through its paces. I don't know if you've ever operated one of those babies, but it beats the hell out of just about any other mode of transportation on a battlefield. The Covenant threw all sorts of things at us: turret emplacements, Banshees, Phantoms. Besides which, we saw another Scarab march by.

Even with all that top-grade UNSC armor around us, getting down that road couldn't have been a narrower thing. We knew we didn't have much time, but I had no idea how fast the clock was ticking. Just when I thought we might have finally made it, a Covenant assault carrier joined the fun and started glassing the city in front of us. This included the highway we were driving on.

Honestly, for a few dark moments, I thought it would wind up like Reach all over again. They'd destroy New Mombasa and then go from there to polish off the entire planet.

I got Mickey on the comm and told him he needed to get that stolen Phantom of ours into the air. "You're coming to us!"

I wouldn't have asked Mickey, Dutch, and Romeo to fly through that crowded sky if we hadn't had Vergil with us. Veronica had mentioned the alien might have the key to winning the entire war stuck somewhere in his circuitry, though, and that seemed like something worth risking all our lives for.

Before they could reach us, though, another Scarab crawled onto the highway and blasted the garbage truck off its wheels. My heart stopped in my chest and didn't start pumping again until I was sure Vergil wasn't going to die then and there and shatter the whole thing apart from the inside—Veronica along with it.

Vergil weathered the storm fine, though, and the Rookie and I got the alien and Veronica out of the truck and hustled them into a nearby building, the public-facing end of the Uplift Nature Reserve. From there, we hung tight, near an open courtyard where our stolen Phantom would have enough room to pick us up.

The Covenant must have been running out of live targets at that point because it seemed like every last one of them that wasn't busy turning the rest of the city into glowing slag was gunning for us. Multiple Phantoms brought wave after wave of angry, well-armed Covenant warriors straight to that courtyard, while artillery fire descended in glowing purple bolts all around us.

The Rookie and I took the battle to the Covenant while Veronica mother-henned Vergil. I shot so many of the invaders that afterward my arms didn't stop vibrating for an hour.

We barely held out until Mickey showed up in our stolen ride. As they hovered over the courtyard, Dutch and Romeo let loose with the plasma cannons on either side of the ship and gunned down every last remaining Covenant soldier in range.

We didn't waste any time hustling onto that Phantom. Vergil gave us a bit of trouble when he panicked at the sight of another Covenant assault cruiser slipping toward us through the Kenyan sky. Gasbags like him don't have much traction, though, and a few good shoves later, we had him up inside our stolen Phantom with the rest of us.

I gotta hand it to Romeo. He was half dead, propping himself up on the mount of the plasma cannon he was firing, but he never gave up. Without him, we might not have made it.

Hell, I could say that about every member of Alpha-Nine, all the way down to the Rookie. I'd even toss Veronica and Vergil into that mix.

Once we got the Huragok calmed down, he took the Phantom's controls. In no time, he had the ship all turboed up and ready to roll, and we were gone.

As far as I know, we were the last humans to make it out of New Mombasa alive. Taking a look out of the Phantom's bay door as we hightailed it out of there, I caught a glimpse of what the Covenant was after. As I found out later, below New Mombasa and spreading out west into Kenya—hidden far below the planet's surface for who knows how long—sat a mighty big machine. Definitely not human in origin. What the machine was and who left it there only made sense much later, but I'm getting ahead of myself again.

Despite the insanity of the moment, or maybe because of it, I had the nerve to ask Veronica about us—her and me—as we left New Mombasa behind.

"Win this war," she said, "then ask me that again."

It was a fair answer, and let me tell you, that's what I call motivation.

NINE

A lpha-Nine had a lot of time to bond together as a team after New Mombasa. Since we'd built up some kind of connection with Vergil, ONI kept us off the front lines for a few weeks. They'd decided that Alpha-Nine could do the most good for the war effort by helping get information out of our pet Engineer instead. Veronica had quarantined us in an orbital ONI station with Vergil, along with a few other alien captives the spooks were trying to keep under wraps and pump for as much information as they could get.

That gave Romeo a chance to heal up, which suited him fine. The rest of us were itching to get back into action, but I have to admit that spending most of my waking moments with Veronica did a lot to improve my mood.

Establishing communications with Vergil was a bit of a trick. Seems the Huragok talk with some kind of sign language so subtle and complicated that most humans can't even recognize it. Still, they seem to be able to understand English well enough, so we can speak to them. It just makes for lopsided conversations and terribly useless interrogations early on.

Of course, they're not called Engineers by accident. Once Vergil had a few spare moments, he figured out a way to talk with us fast. He scrounged up a tablet and programmed it so that he could make words appear on it with but a touch of a cilia-covered tentacle. Later he even rigged up a speaker and a speech-to-text program to give himself a voice. Apparently, other Huragok elsewhere used a similar setup to do the same—or so I'm told.

Despite that, he didn't like to use it. He'd been a Covenant slave from the moment he came into the world, and even though he'd been brave enough to revolt against them, the thought of them still out there terrified him. Getting him to open up about the Covenant's plans took a lot of time—and a bit of help.

He was happy enough to chat about things other than the Covenant, and we passed a lot of time that way. I discovered that the Huragok name their young by the way they find their balance after they're born or created or hatched or printed or whatever. Vergil's real name was Quick to Adjust, which I suppose said a lot about him as an adult, too. But that moniker was enough of a mouthful that we simply stuck with calling him Vergil instead.

Turns out the original Vergil—at least in this case—was a subroutine in the Superintendent program that ran New Mombasa's infrastructure. You know, things like traffic lights, train schedules, water releases, tollbooths, and so on. It wasn't one of those fancy AIs with a full-on personality like the ones you sometimes see running warships for the UNSC, but a much simpler variety—in other words, just a complex program that did a complex job.

The guy in charge of that AI—Dr. Daniel Endesha—was a widower too busy helping run New Mombasa to watch over his daughter, Sadie, so he programmed Vergil to do it for him. No matter where she was in the city, or what she was doing, Vergil kept an eye on Sadie, and if anything went wrong, he alerted Dr. Endesha at once. I'm no father, but I can see the appeal of a system like that.

When Quick to Adjust downloaded what was left of the

Superintendent after the Covenant invasion, he wound up with Vergil inside him, too, and their personalities kind of merged. Well, maybe more their *purposes*.

Maybe that's one reason Quick to Adjust was more willing to work with the UNSC than most other Engineers. He just so happened to download the right information to make him just a little more human.

Despite everything, we didn't make a whole lot of headway with getting Covenant secrets out of Vergil at first. We were able to copy data from the Superintendent off him—with his help, of course—but we knew he had more to offer. He was too scared to give it up, though, until we got a visit from one of the Master Chief's old friends.

Working with Vergil took a lot of patience, but the clock was ticking faster every day. The Covenant had found something under New Mombasa, and the UNSC needed to know what it was and what it could do.

It was an enigma that might help us win the war. For one thing, the fact that it was buried on Earth seemed to be the only thing holding the Covenant back from glassing the entire planet. If we could at least stop the Covenant from making off with it, we could keep Earth—and all of humanity's hopes for it—alive.

And if we could figure it out and take control of it ourselves? Well, some people thought that might turn the entire tide.

Try as we might, we couldn't pry it out of Vergil for anything though. No amount of cajoling, pleading, and even begging would get him to open up about it.

Charming Romeo even threatened to puncture the gasbag while I conveniently had Veronica out of the way for a while. That didn't do a bit of good. It just made Vergil clam up tighter than ever when Romeo walked his way.

We did manage to wheedle a few things out of him. Just enough to make sure High Command kept him on the station. We learned, for instance, that he could tap into the Covenant battlenet—or at least parts of it that he knew how to hack into. He somehow managed it remotely—from on our secret ONI space station—in a way we didn't quite understand.

When I say "we," I include the ONI scientists in the group, who were studying Vergil on the sly. They analyzed everything about him from his odor to the kinds of radio waves he emitted. Honestly, no one in Alpha-Nine had the slightest shot at figuring any of that out. We're the blunt end of the UNSC stick.

It wasn't until Admiral Hood—the very head of the UNSC Navy himself—sent Sergeant Major Avery Johnson to the space station for a friendly chat with the Huragok that we got him to open up. Johnson turned out to know more about the Engineers than everyone else on the station put together. A lot more.

"The Brutes," he said as he sat down on a crate that put him at the same level as all six of Vergil's blinking eyes. "The bastards who put bombs on your buddies and killed millions of my people, they're digging a mighty big hole."

Even after a month of the Covenant poking around in that hole, no one in the UNSC knew exactly what they were after, or what that ancient machine they'd found could actually do. But every one of us in that room—Johnson included—suspected Vergil did.

Later, I found out that Johnson was pretty certain the Ark—or at least something that led to it—had been buried underneath New Mombasa. He wanted Vergil to confirm that for him and, if possible, tell him what the hell that meant the UNSC was getting into.

"You're gonna tell me exactly what they're looking for. And then, you're gonna help me stop them." I tell you, I wouldn't want to have played poker against Johnson, ever. The man was born to be a drill sergeant.

Once Vergil finally opened up, ONI didn't need Alpha-Nine around much anymore, and they set us loose so we could get back to the war.

That cut my little working vacation with Veronica short, but by that time, we'd come to an understanding. Much as we cared for each other, two working soldiers couldn't commit to anything in the middle of a war.

Such plans are for peacetime. Or so we told ourselves.

Doing the smart thing didn't mean it didn't hurt though.

"Hey," I said, "Gretchen and Dutch got hitched."

"Gretchen was sidelined by an injury," she said. "And Dutch is stuck here with Alpha-Nine rather than back home with her. Is that how you want us to be?"

"I could retire," I said, looking for some kind of solution that would make us both happy. "Maybe we both could."

She didn't buy it for a second. She gazed into my eyes with a look that said *I know you too well*. "Not while there's still a job we need to do," she said.

One of the things I love about Veronica is how she's always right. But I wouldn't be honest if I didn't confess I sometimes hate it, too.

I heard later that the information Vergil provided gave us the edge we needed to save humanity. That's a whole 'nother story, and to be honest, I hear the Master Chief did most of the heavy lifting. If you want to know the gory details, you'll have to ask someone else and show them you have the proper clearance.

Anyhow, it turns out the Forerunners hadn't buried the Ark beneath the city, but it was something nearly as good: a transdimensional portal that led right to it. Seems like it had been there since we weren't much more than cave people digging around in the dirt, and we'd had no idea the entire time.

I'm not sure I want to think a whole lot about what that says about the origins of humanity. Or about how good we are at knowing what's under our feet.

Either way, we're still here, and the Covenant's been shattered. I guess it doesn't matter if you win ugly, just so long as you win.

TEN

After New Mombasa, I kind of lost track of Vergil. Part of that was the fact he was one of ONI's best-kept secrets. The other was that he was a manufactured alien who'd been part of the Covenant, which meant we didn't have a whole lot in common. Other than the trauma bond we shared from surviving the fall of a major Earth city together, that is.

Plus, there was still a war on, and I had other things to worry about. Like keeping me and my team alive long enough to kill as many Covenant soldiers as we could manage.

Every now and then, Veronica would update me on Vergil's status. In an unofficial way.

He was, as you might imagine, one of the secret heroes of the Covenant War. Not only could he tap into the Covenant battle-net for us, but he was great at figuring out all sorts of Forerunner artifacts that the UNSC ran across. Basic things that might stump our human scientists for months—like how to turn a device on—he already knew about. Having him gave us a fantastic edge.

I already told you that he could fix just about anything, too. Not that he got much of a chance to take on challenges like that over what little time there was left in the war. He was too valuable an asset to risk on a battlefield.

And after the war ended, about a month-and-a-half following the events in New Mombasa, ONI kept Vergil under wraps. Even with the Covenant broken, he had plenty of work to do for us. It wasn't like the Brutes and the Elites just walked away and settled back into peaceful lives, treaties or no. They'd been a part of the Covenant for countless generations. They didn't have any frame of reference for living for anything but war.

I understand ONI mostly kept Vergil busy continuing to puzzle out Forerunner artifacts. Now that we could poke around more of the galaxy without fear of our worlds being glassed, we were turning up a lot more of these things.

So when—about three years later, I'll say?—Veronica disclosed that Vergil had been kidnapped on the planet Talitsa, along with Sadie Endesha, I didn't even give it a second thought. I jumped right at the job. That put her back on her heels, which I'll admit, I enjoyed plenty. She was a hard woman to surprise.

This was now in 2555, long after Romeo, Mickey, and me had become Spartans.

Yeah, I know. At this point you're probably wondering whatever happened to "my answer is no"? Just bear with me—I'm getting to that. There's a method to my madness.

Where was I? Oh, right. Veronica.

She and I had become a lot closer since the official end of the Covenant War, but despite that, we both remained dedicated to our jobs.

"No arguments?" she'd said. "No comebacks?"

I shook my head with an emphatic *no.* "If Vergil's in trouble, then Alpha-Nine is on it. Well, what's left of us, anyhow."

"You almost sound like you're maturing."

"I just figure you have your reasons for sending us after him, and I trust that you're right."

"Wait, you *are* maturing."

"I like to think of it more as surrendering to your wisdom."

She grabbed me by the chin then and looked me straight in the eyes. "Are you feeling all right?"

I shrugged. "It's been a long time since I've seen Vergil. It'll be a good chance to catch up. After we rescue him, of course." That actually wasn't a lie. In the weeks we'd spent in orbit with the Huragok, I'd grown to know him better than any other non-human I'd ever known, including my family dog.

She gave me a disbelieving frown. "Sometimes I think those Spartan treatments messed with more than just your body."

I favored her with a wry smile. "I'm sure you'd know more about that than me." I hesitated for a moment. "You think he'll still recognize me? Or any of us?"

"You're still you, aren't you? Spartan or not?"

"I'd say so, but I don't exactly have the full-on Engineer's perspective. What do you think?"

I held out my arms as an invitation to examine me. They stretched farther now than they had for my entire adulthood, which still felt strange to me. Like I'd gone through some kind of second adolescence and come out of it a new kind of adult.

Maybe that's why they tapped kids for the previous Spartan programs. It's hard enough to go through those kinds of changes once. That way, they went straight from kids to superhumans.

With us ODST guys, we already knew how hard puberty had been. Becoming a Spartan as an adult is something like that, only far worse. This time around, you realize you volunteered for the experience, and you can only hope that you'll recognize yourself when you come out on the far end of it.

I hadn't been a Spartan for all that long at that point, and I'll admit to still having a few butterflies about it. Veronica looked me up and down and gave me an approving nod. "You'll do fine."

I caressed her shoulder. "Too bad you're still just a spook, huh?"

She punched me flat in the stomach, hard. Back in my ODST days, that would have doubled me over. The lady's got a hell of a right hook. Now, though, I barely felt it. It bounced off my reengineered abs, and she yowled in surprise as she tried to shake the pain out of her hand.

"You're lucky I'm just a spook," she said. "Or I'd have no use for you at all."

"Oh, I'm sure you'd think of something," I said. "You're one of the most resourceful people I know."

"They taught you flattery in Spartan school, too?"

"Well, I already knew how to shoot."

I couldn't help needling her a bit. By then she'd already given me plenty of proof that, when it came to me joining the Spartans, she enjoyed the results.

She hadn't been quite so supportive when I'd turned down my first chance to join them, two years earlier.

In fact, she'd wasted a lot of our remaining vacation time on Sundown trying to get me to change my mind.

"Just think of all the good you could do," she'd said. She didn't see why I'd passed up such a blessing.

"Would you have taken Jun up on that?" I asked. "I mean, if he'd asked you?"

"You're damn right I would have." More than a hint of jealousy colored her reply. "I wouldn't even have waited for them to ask. If I was a soldier, I'd have tracked the new Spartan program down and camped outside of their door until they gave me a chance to beg for the transformation."

She liked to think that all her badgering of me about fulfilling my responsibilities and living up to my potential had some effect. And maybe it did a little, if I'm honest.

But I didn't decide to take the plunge and join the Spartans because of her, much as I might have let her think that sometimes. It happened because of another woman.

Sarah Palmer.

ELEVEN

You have to understand that I hadn't seen Sarah Palmer for years after that rescue on Sargasso back in '46. Hell, I didn't even think much about her in all that time. I was too busy fighting the war, during which I lost far more friends than I care to think about. People who were much closer to me.

I didn't have a lot of time to spare for soldiers I'd saved. I never felt like I'd done anything heroic. It was all just part of the job.

Back home on Draco III, when I was fishing with my uncle Lou, a member of our crew fell into the open sea. Fortunately, she'd been wearing the required safety line, but we all knew that didn't matter much. As fast as our boat was moving, it was like she was water-skiing beneath the waves. There was no way she'd ever be able to pull herself back up to safety.

I grabbed her line, which was as taut as steel wire, and kept it from flopping around all over the back of the boat, which could have cut her loose. Uncle Lou took one of the cables we used to haul in catches and hooked it to the woman's line. He started up the winch right after that, and soon we had her back on deck.

She was wet as an ice shark, and had stopped breathing to boot. I quickly leaned on her chest until she coughed up half the sea, and she then sat straight up as if a jellyfish had stung her in her rump. After that, Uncle Lou and I took her belowdecks and turned her over to the first mate. Then we went right back to work.

At dinner that night, I wanted to talk about it, but Uncle Lou just waved me off. *Don't make no big deal out of it*, he said. *Wasn't nothing to it. You fell over, and she'd have done the same for you. Anyone on this boat would.*

I looked around the mess and saw he was right. I didn't know the names of half the people on board that fishing barge, but I'd have busted my ass to save any one of them. And I could count on them to step up if I was the one in need.

It was the same thing as being a marine. I couldn't tell you how many people I saved over the years. Not in the glad-you-had-my-back kind of way, but in the I'd-have-died-for-sure sort.

But maybe just as many people saved me. There were lots of times I know it happened, and probably just as many more that I didn't. When you're in the middle of a firefight, you don't stop to say thanks, and you surely don't keep score.

Every time I went out in the field with Alpha-Nine, we covered each other as best we could. Most times, we all came back alive, and that's when we knew we'd done our jobs well.

But not always. The times you blow it—or when you let one of your pals make their last mistake—those are the ones you remember. Doesn't matter if it's your fault or not.

That's a long way of saying that, after Alpha-Nine saved Sarah Palmer on Sargasso back in 2546, I didn't expect a word of thanks from her the next time we met. Maybe I'd get a grateful nod of acknowledgment, showing that she recognized me and remembered what I'd done. That was more than I'd figured.

Believe it or not, that leads me right back around to what happened with the Rookie.

I know. It's a convoluted tale. I'm a complex guy.

So, eight years later, in 2554, when Alpha-Nine was stuck in the legislative chambers on Draco III—with United Rebel Front Captain Ingridson holding a gun to the Rookie's head—the last voice I expected to hear over the comm to shatter my concentration was Palmer's.

"Gunnery Sergeant Buck? This is Spartan Sarah Palmer. I understand you're having some problems. We're here to help."

"*Spartan* Sarah Palmer?" I couldn't hide my surprise, but I didn't have time for this. If we didn't resolve this hostage situation fast and well, the Rookie was going to die.

I signaled Mickey and Dutch to slip out of the legislature's main floor, get upstairs, and circle back around to the balcony where Ingridson was holding the Rookie hostage. They moved out as quiet as ghosts.

Romeo hung back with me. He hefted his grenades again, but I waved him off once more.

"New and improved, Gunny," Palmer was saying over the conn. "My fireteam has a lock on your location. We can be there in under a minute and assist you with your situation."

"Negative, Palmer. The op's gone delicate on us. We got this."

I don't know why I turned her down. Maybe it was what Veronica said about the Spartans being a blunt instrument. Maybe I was afraid they'd barge in and get the Rookie killed.

I hate to think it had something to do with the resentment most every Helljumper has for the Spartans. That would be damn stupid. But I can't rule it out.

"It's your op, Buck. We're on standby for you until we get the all clear."

"Copy that." I was about to say more, but Captain Ingridson interrupted me.

"This is not a negotiation!" the Front leader shouted. She

removed her pistol from the Rookie's head and put a bullet into his knee instead.

The Rookie screamed in pain and twisted around like a lashed-down lion, but the soldiers holding him up didn't loosen their grip.

"Come on out now, troopers!" yelled Ingridson. "Surrender, or we'll kill your fascist friend here and now!"

Sick of waiting for orders from me, Romeo stood up and fired a burst at Ingridson. The rounds glanced off the almost invisible shield protecting the presidential balcony, ricocheting in every direction.

"Goddammit, Romeo!" I barked at him. "Knock that shit off!"

He dropped back behind cover, snarling with frustration like a caged dog who couldn't quite reach a raw steak. I growled right back at him. We were going to have a short, brutal talk about waiting for orders when this was over.

Ingridson just laughed off the pointless attack. Like some kind of cheap video villain. And then she put her gun back at the Rookie's head.

"I'm tired of playing this game with you," Ingridson said. "I'm counting to three."

I didn't see any other route out. She had us cold. Even if I'd called in the Spartans at that point, the woman would have shot the Rookie dead the moment they burst into the place. I only had one call to make here, so I made it.

I stood up from behind the desk I'd been using as cover and held my hands up in as casual a way as I could manage. "No need for that."

"Drop your gun!"

I let the pistol in my hand fall to the ground. I still had my M7S submachine gun magnetically latched to my back, but I had no chance of reaching that before Ingridson could empty her gun, and she knew it.

I gestured at Romeo to do the same. He complied, but maybe only because he knew how much I was going to chew him out later for jumping the gun on me. He stood next to me and dumped his weapon at his feet.

"I didn't know the balcony was shielded," he said with the barest hint of an apology in his voice.

"It's the seat of a colonial government," I replied. "You think we're primitives?"

"I, for one, am glad to see one of you showing a little initiative," Ingridson said before Romeo could muster an answer. "For the most part, you damn Helljumpers are all the same. You follow your orders like good little soldiers, never questioning who gives them to you and why."

"It's a living," I said.

I don't think she appreciated the joke.

"For you! What about the innocents you kill?"

"I didn't think most of the bugs I killed were innocent."

"That war is over," Ingridson said. "Go home!"

That's when I did something that surprised her. I took off my helmet.

"I *am* home," I said. "My name's Eddie Buck. I was born right here at Draco Mercy, New Albany, Lombard, Draco III. Lived most of my life in Karnak before I enlisted to go save humanity."

That sure as hell shut her big mouth for the moment. I'm sure she had a whole speech of revolutionary, isolationist rhetoric ready to go, but my guess is most of it relied on making me feel guilty for invading this privacy-loving colony whose only crime was wanting to be left out of galactic politics.

"I know," I said. "It's hard to believe anyone would want to leave such a peaceful place behind." I made pointed glances at the blast and bullet marks that scarred the legislative chamber.

"We're trying to rebuild in the ashes of the war the UNSC started with the Covenant!"

"Ah!" I said, appalled but not surprised. "Is that the latest line of bullshit you're trying to feed people around here? Can't make them forget about how the Covenant glassed half the planet and then sent their infantry down here to feed on the survivors—so you're going to blame all that on the UNSC instead?"

"The people need to hear the truth."

"And so you deliver the truth to them with bullets?" I held my helmet over my heart. "I'm a native son, Captain. Give me your spiel. Convince me I should be standing over there with you rather than down here. Just— I want you to do it without hurting anyone."

Palmer spoke to me then over the comm in my helmet. "How's it going down there, Buck?"

I didn't dare answer. I was sure Ingridson couldn't hear Palmer from where she was, but I'd either have to put my helmet back on or shout into it to get any kind of message through.

She was a professional though. She wouldn't dive in without my say-so—not like Romeo had. I hoped.

But Ingridson didn't get to call herself a captain in her Front cell because she was an idiot. She knew what I was doing.

"Quit stalling," she finally said. "Bring your other armed thugs out to join you, or I'll not only kill this man . . ." She pointed her gun at my unhelmeted head. "I'll kill you, too."

Romeo snorted. "Doesn't that force field work both ways?"

I glared at him. "Do I look like I installed it?"

Ingridson squeezed off a shot at Romeo. It caught him in his faceplate and knocked him to the floor.

I don't know how that particular one-way force field operated. Maybe it was constructed so things could pass through from one direction but not the other. Maybe it was rigged to blink off and on at the pull of a trigger inside the balcony. Maybe she just poked the barrel of her pistol through it before she fired.

All I know is that she could hurt us, and we couldn't return the favor.

I went to help Romeo up and instantly thought better of it.

"Fair enough," I said, turning back to Ingridson. "You're holding all the cards. What's your play?"

"Get off our planet."

"*Our?*" I arched an eyebrow at her.

"The people here need loyalists like me to look out for them, not traitors like you."

I ignored the jab. "I get it. You think you're doing something to help the people of Draco. This isn't the way to do it."

"And the UNSC has a better way?"

"Buck?" Palmer said through my helmet. "We're detecting more hostiles closing on your position."

That meant Ingridson was using the same tactics on me as I was on her. She was playing for time until her own reinforcements could reach us, but she'd called me on my stalling to keep me from getting suspicious about hers.

In other circumstances, I could have grown to like her.

I flashed her a winning smile and shrugged. "We saved the galaxy from the Covenant. I'd say that's a point in our favor."

"For all the good it did the people of Draco."

That stung more than I cared to admit. I'd been angry about the fall of Draco III, too, but I'd known whom to blame for it. "The UNSC didn't invade here. You'd blame the victim for the crime?"

"I blame the filthy racketeer who promises protection and isn't around to supply it when you need it most."

Okay, that tore it for me.

I launched into that self-righteous coward, stabbing my finger at her to punctuate every accusation. "And where the hell were *you* when the Covenant burned this place to glass? Where were *you* when they sent their soldiers to hunt down my family and friends? *Where were you when those unholy bastards ate my sister and her little kids?*"

My red-faced rant sent Ingridson's blood straight to her cheeks. And for just a distracted moment, she lowered her gun.

"Gunny?" Dutch said over the comm. "We're in position."

I shouted right into my helmet. "Alpha-Nine! Go!"

I dove to the left, jamming my helmet back on my head as I hit the ground.

Ingridson started to empty her pistol at me. One of the slugs caught me in the arm, sending me spinning into the desks and chairs arranged in a semicircle facing the balcony.

My armor took the worst of it, but a chunk of the bullet found its way through the protection and buried itself in my shoulder. The impact felt even worse, like getting kicked by a Brute.

"Clear!" Dutch said over the comm while the bullets were still flying. An instant later, an explosion at the doors leading up to the balcony interrupted Ingridson's furious barrage.

I grabbed at my shoulder and guessed by the fact that I could still feel it that I might survive. "We're hot, Palmer!" I said into the comm. "Cover our backs?"

"Already engaging the incoming Front troops," the Spartan said, calm as ever. "Wouldn't leave you hanging."

I leaped to my feet, unslinging my SMG as I went. As I stood, I saw Mickey charging onto the balcony. He brought his rifle up to bear on Ingridson and shouted at the top of his lungs, *"Hold it right there!"*

The Front leader already had her gun back at the Rookie's head. I'm sure the way she saw it, she had only one play.

Even if she managed to survive this encounter, we'd capture her for sure. Her life as a rebel was over. The best she could expect was a long prison sentence punctuated by intense periods of inter-rogation.

I can't say she would've been wrong about that.

In her mind, she wasn't getting out of there alive. By choice. That wasn't the kind of life she wanted.

And if she was going down, then she was taking as many of us with her as she could. Even if that was only one.

She pulled the trigger on the Rookie, and his brains blew out of the back of his skull in a fine red mist that scattered all over the legislature's floor. Then he crumpled backward, tumbling over the balcony's railing. His body slammed right on the podium from which Draco III's legislators gave speeches to the rest of the world. It splintered under his weight.

Mickey could only stand there in shock and gape at what In-gridson had done. While he stared in horror, Dutch spun in be-hind him and opened up at the rebels with his shotgun. In close quarters like that, it hit all three of them at once.

Captain Ingridson took the brunt of the buckshot in her chest. She went flying down after the Rookie, landing on the marble floor just beyond him. She skidded a couple more meters, leaving a bright red smear behind her.

Dutch's shot didn't catch the other two rebel soldiers hard enough to knock them flat. He immediately took out the one on the right with a second shot. The one on the left threw himself to his knees and tossed his hands into the air.

"Don't shoot!" he shouted, his voice cracking in desperation and fear. "Please! I give up!"

Mickey pointed his rifle at the man's head. Even from down on the main floor, I could see his barrel shaking. For a second, I thought he was going to kill an unarmed foe. Much as I wanted justice for the Rookie, if such a thing was possible to find, we'd gotten it the moment Dutch killed Captain Ingridson—an eye for an eye. She was an active, armed threat—one who'd just murdered an unarmed ODST in cold blood—and no one would have found fault with Dutch's actions.

Shooting a man trying to surrender, though, was something entirely different.

"Mickey!" I shouted into the comm. "Stand down! Right goddamn now!"

The urgency and authority in my voice brought him up short. He took a step back, still trembling, and Dutch stepped between him and the kneeling rebel.

"Check your corners!" I said.

Romeo and I scanned the edges of the legislative chamber while Mickey, still shaken, looked out into the hallway outside of the balcony. Dutch kept his shotgun on the terrified rebel.

"Down on your face!" he barked at the man. "Now!"

The rebel complied. Everything grew quiet for a moment, and I could hear gunshots somewhere else inside the building, getting closer.

"Palmer?" I said. "We got a man down! How's it going out there?"

"Hold tight," she said. "We're coming in."

"What's your ETA?"

The doors at the back of the chamber blew open in a cloud of dust and debris. In walked an entire fireteam of Spartans dressed in red and silver armor.

The one in the lead stripped off her helmet and shook free her hair. I recognized Palmer in an instant. She gave me a grim smile filled with satisfaction rather than happiness.

"How's about now?"

TWELVE

We buried the Rookie at sea the following week. The UNSC is great at a lot of things, but they don't usually handle the repatriation of remains back to the deceased's home planet. For one, it's too busy sending living troops into war zones to spare the resources to ship the dead ones in the opposite direction. And two, it's not always easy to find enough remains to send home. No disrespect intended, but it's foolish and bittersweet to risk living soldiers to gather their fallen comrades.

Romeo, Dutch, and Mickey were there for the ceremony, of course; all of us in our dress blues at just after the crack of dawn. An honor guard loaded the Rookie's black coffin into an old Albatross dropship and draped both UEG and ODST flags over his remains with all the respect the man deserved. Then the three of us climbed into the bird, sat in the seats closest to the Rookie, and settled in for the ride.

We didn't say much to each other. It was a warm, beautiful day, and we left the dropship's side doors open. The honor guard had secured the flags to the coffin so they wouldn't go sailing away. We'd been on countless missions with the Rookie just like that, staring out the panoramic doors as the thrumming winds battered us.

We took off from the main port in New Albany and flew

low out over the city. I'd gotten a high-altitude view of it as we'd come in for the assault on the captured capitol building, but it had looked a lot like an aerial photograph. Even from there, the vastness of the damage the Covenant had inflicted on the city had been easy to see, but it had been like looking at a distant mountain range.

Now, scudding barely over the rooftops, the destruction seemed far more personal. You could pick out the individual streets that had been destroyed, houses that had been bombed out, even places where the corpses had been burned.

It was a relief when we reached the shore. The ocean's waves hadn't changed one bit. This part, at least, still felt like home.

The pilot kept going straight out to sea until we couldn't see land on any side. We could have been on any of a number of watery planets, maybe even back on Earth.

I knew Draco's oceans too well to fool myself that way though. The color of the water, the way the sun glinted off the waves, the scent of the breeze.

It felt right.

I stood up to show that we'd gotten to the burial spot, and the pilot hauled the dropship's engines back until we came to a gentle stop, hovering over some random point.

We gathered around the Rookie's coffin and stared down at it.

"Why we got to do this?" Romeo said.

I backhanded him across the shoulder. "Show some respect."

"He don't mean nothing by it, Gunny," Dutch said. "It's just— you ever have a show like this for anyone else?"

I realized what they meant then. I'd lost a lot of friends in the war, including every member of Alpha-Nine since I'd taken command, with the exception of the three guys standing there with me. We'd never had a funeral for any of them.

"Well, we haven't lost anyone since the war ended," I said. "This is one of the perks of peace."

"Peace." Romeo snorted. "I liked it better when they called it what it was."

Mickey just stared at the coffin the entire time. The rest of us joined him.

"You were a good soldier, Rookie," I said to the capsule of black plastic underneath the flags. "I was proud to serve with you. I'm glad you got to see the end of the war, which started before you were born. I just wish you'd gotten to go back home, too." I looked around at the others. "Anyone else want to say something?"

None of them moved forward. They all looked like I felt: stricken, frustrated, and maybe a little bit angry, too.

Seeing neither Mickey nor Dutch was ready to move, Romeo shrugged and then nodded down at the body. "It only takes one mistake, kid. You went a long time before you made it."

With that ice broken, Dutch knelt down and put his hand on the burial capsule. He held his tongue for a long moment before he spoke in a low voice. "Lord, I don't know if I can do this anymore."

"Just tell him good-bye," Romeo said. "No need to get all weepy about it."

"He's not talking about the funeral," I said.

Dutch bowed his head. "Yeah. I'm done. I'm putting in for a transfer as soon as we're finished here."

"I thought we went over this." Romeo looked like Dutch had just hamstrung him from behind. "What the hell else you going to do with yourself? The only thing you know how to do is soldiering."

"I used to drive road-trains," Dutch said. "Maybe I can go back to that."

"So you're going to go back to hauling groceries?"

Dutch shrugged. "I don't know. Either way, it's time for a

change. My wife mustered out last year. She's been waiting for me to join her."

"Yeah, well, Gretchen was ODST, too. She knows why we have to do what we do. She knows how important it is."

Dutch looked his old pal in the eye. "I don't disagree with that. But the war's over. I've pulled my weight. I've worked my share. Screw it. It's time for someone else to step up."

Romeo looked shellshocked. I didn't know if he was going to shove Dutch out of the transport with the Rookie or sit down and cry. Instead, he put out his hand to his friend, who took it, and he hauled him up into a bear hug. "You make sure she takes good care of you," he said.

"What about you?" Dutch said with real concern as they broke their embrace.

Romeo laughed it off and pounded a thick finger into his own chest. "Whatever. Never worry about the man on *this* end of my gun."

As they chuckled, I relaxed just a bit and turned toward Mickey. He hadn't said a word the entire time. "Hey. How about you?"

Mickey shook his head. "I'm staying." His voice was as raw as if he'd been shouting over a gunfight since the moment he woke up.

"I meant, anything you want to say for the Rookie."

He clammed up tighter than ever.

"Okay, suit yourself."

Dutch put a hand on Mickey's shoulder. "You can't blame yourself for this."

"Sure he can," said Romeo. I shot the man a look that could have peeled the laminate off his armor, but he kept on going. "If he hadn't hesitated when he came through that door, we'd all be blasting out of here on our way to our next mission instead of saying our adioses."

Dutch winced. "That ain't fair. I was right there—"

The next thing I know, Romeo was on the floor of the transport with blood streaming out of his nose, and I was hauling Mickey off him and pinning him against the far bulkhead. "Enough! Stand down!"

Mickey shoved back against me, and I lost it. "I said *stand down*, goddammit, or I'll toss you right out of this craft!"

"And we ain't going to have one of these little parties for you!" Romeo said. Dutch was trying to settle him down and had already ripped open a pack of gauze to help staunch his pal's bleeding nose.

The fight went out of Mickey right after that. I put him on one side of the craft and Romeo on the other. Dutch came over and lent me a hand, and we gave the Rookie's capsule the little shove it needed to topple out of the transport and disappear into the waves below.

We didn't say much on the way back.

It bothered me a bit that no one else had been at the funeral besides us three. The Rookie had been born on Luna, in Crisium City, Naniwa. Most if not all of his relatives had died during the Covenant's assault on the home system back in 2552. Some of the bugs had decided to scour the Moon while they were on their way to Earth, if only to make sure that we couldn't launch any kind of sneak attack from our bases there. A bunch of the home colonies got hit pretty hard when the Covies came through—Luna and Mars in particular—but all of them fared better than Earth.

He hadn't wanted to talk too much about it. When I asked him, he just gritted his teeth and said, "There's nothing left there for me now."

Like many marines, he'd dedicated his life to the UNSC. He no longer had any family outside.

I might have ignored that and tried to hunt down someone on Luna who knew him, but I didn't much see the point. No one was going to come all the way out here to Draco III to say their farewells.

I might have invited local friends and family of my own to the Rookie's funeral, to fill out the ranks a bit if nothing else, but I didn't have any left either. Most of the people who'd been some-place else when the planet got glassed were UNSC, too, and few of us liked going back to see what had happened to our homeworld.

Mind you, the new colonists had done a remarkable job with the place since the war had ended, but they hadn't rebuilt much outside of New Albany. Some folks who liked the isolation had set up camp in the more remote spots of the planet, starting over from scratch. Others had reclaimed long-abandoned places, hoping no heirs ever showed up to reclaim them.

Feeling low about the Rookie when we got back to New Albany, I hopped the next civilian flight out to Karnak to go on a tour of the places I knew as a kid. I hadn't been back in more than twenty-five years, but the memories of it flooded over at me.

Sure, technically I was forty-four at the time, but I'd spent more of those years off-world in cryosleep than I cared to add up. In terms of mileage, though, I'd rolled up more of that than any-one I'd known before I signed up to fight the Covenant.

When I got to the tiny airport in Karnak, I rented myself a car and went for a drive. As I walked across the open parking lot to the rental, I stopped for a moment to soak it all in.

Standing there in Draco III's light in civvies brought those early years right back to me. I could close my eyes and imagine that nothing had changed, that I could drive to my old neighbor-hood, slide down my old street, turn into my driveway, and have my mom there ready to welcome me home.

The sun on my face felt the exact same way it had all those years ago. One thing they don't tell you about when you sign up for the UNSC is that every sun is unique. Sure, the ones we can tolerate under an open atmosphere share a lot of the same characteristics, but they differ, too, mostly in small ways.

Their intensity. Their warmth. Their hue.

Every sun has its own kind of burn, and I knew Draco's better than any. The sensation of its radiation dancing on my skin made me smile.

But the planet's smell? That was something else entirely.

The Covenant had trashed Draco III about nine years ago. The planet had bounced back some from that. No matter what humanity does, nature marches on, as my dad used to say. Fair enough, but nature also takes its time, and nine years isn't enough to recover from a Covenant glassing.

The brittle black shit on the outskirts of the huge swathes of destruction the Covenant leaves behind isn't actually glass, of course. It's what you get when you melt everything in the area into a chemical soup and let it cool and harden on its own—more like obsidian from a volcano than anything else.

Most colonies aren't built on volcanically active planets. We prefer easier targets for terraforming, meaning you don't wind up with things like obsidian just lying around.

Not until the Covenant comes your way.

I tried to make it into my old neighborhood. Glass blocked the way in. The entire area had been flattened into a black, hardened sea dozens of klicks wide. And this was just the edge of the destruction, far from ground zero.

Glass doesn't form smoothly underfoot. It's not like you could strap on some skates and set up an old Earth hockey game on it. Not everything melts well, even under the Covenant's relentless plasma bombardment, so you get things sticking up out of the glass here and there. Mostly they're internal scaffolding for high-rise buildings, but you can find other things, especially at the edges of a blast.

It takes longer than you'd think for the glass to cool entirely as well. I could actually see white-capped waves in the spot where I guessed my old house would have been. I like to think of that as some last act of courage. Pointless, sure, but defiant to the end.

I decided to wind my way around toward where Uncle Lou used to moor his boat. The boat was gone, but by some fluke, this part of my old stomping grounds hadn't been glassed. Someone had gone to the trouble to clean up the docks, but the surrounding area hadn't seen the same kind of love.

Leeward's was still open.

It's an old dive bar that Uncle Lou used to take me to after a long day on the sea. I was too young to drink, but we ate there regularly. Uncle Lou and my dad threw me a hell of a going away party there the night before I had to report to the UNSC. I was still ruined when I staggered into the recruiter's office.

Leeward's served an amazing chowder filled with all sorts of seafood that I never wanted anyone to name for fear of wrecking it for me. It came out of this huge pot that probably hadn't been cleaned since the founding of the colony. Every time it ran low, they just tossed more water and fleshy sea creature bits into it, along with a little spice, and kept it going.

Damn, it was good. Made my mouth water just thinking about it.

The front of the place still bore bullet holes and plasma scars. It kind of added to its charm. At least they'd cleaned up the blood.

The inside looked like someone had gutted it from stem to stern and then gotten bored with the refurb and just started tossing tables and stools into it until it felt more like a bar. The place stood empty except for a couple of retired fishers who were old enough to prefer talking about the sea to actually being on it. I didn't recognize the bartender, but that wasn't any surprise either.

After a bit of chitchat, I started in on a bottle of some local-made *baijiu*. I didn't have any plans to stop.

I'd worked through about half of it by the time Jun found me there. He didn't say a word. Just sat down next to me until I noticed him.

I signaled the bartender for another glass and poured Jun a tall one. He gave it a dubious sniff and wrinkled his nose at it, but I had to give him credit for not letting his eyes water at the smell.

He raised his glass to me, and I clinked mine against his.

"To the Rookie," I said.

He said nothing in return.

After he finished his drink, I poured him another. He tried to wave me off, but I ignored the gesture.

"Don't worry about your manners," I said. "This isn't a polite place."

"I'm happy to toast your fallen friend," Jun said. "But that's not why I'm here."

I grunted at that. "You going to take the Rookie's place in Alpha-Nine?"

He smiled. "I'm a long way past active duty, I'm afraid."

"Must be nice."

"It has its ups and downs."

I sighed, put down my drink, and looked him in the eye. "So let's cut to the good part. My answer's the same as before."

"But you haven't heard my offer."

I raised my eyebrows. "Oh, there's an *offer* this time? All I remember is you hunting around for my sense of patriotism."

"And I found it, right there underneath your loyalty to your troopers, which trumped it."

"And I still have troopers." Maybe not as many as I'd had that morning, which he probably already knew. But that was beside the point.

"For now."

I squinted hard at him. "Explain that."

Active combat or not, Jun was still a Spartan-III. He towered over me, even sitting down. I had no doubt he would wipe the bar with me in a fistfight, wring me out, and then ask the bartender if he could go ahead and clean up the floor as well. Still, I had to grip the bar's brass railing white-knuckle tight to keep myself from taking a half-drunken swing at him.

"Easy, Gunny," Jun said. "No one's taking your team away from you."

I relaxed my grip on the railing. I'd been wondering if I could rip it from the bar and bash him with it before he tied it around me like a bow. "Then why don't you cut the bullshit and get to the point."

Jun held up his hands. "You made your complaints clear the last time around."

"Did Veronica put you up to this?"

"She didn't have to. I like to keep track of my failures."

"You sure know how to sweet-talk a guy."

"Of the very limited number of people I approached about joining the first class of Spartan-IVs, you're one of an even tinier number that turned me down."

"You mean I'm still the only one?"

"Yes."

I made a show of looking around. "Is this your way of making me feel like a jackass for letting such a golden opportunity to serve humanity slip me by?"

"Not my original intent. That's just a side effect. If that's how it makes you feel, though, I'll admit to taking a bit of personal pleasure in it."

"How kind of you."

"I'm a good judge of character, Buck. Add in the fact that I have a cutting-edge AI on my side, and it's rare that I make a mistake about someone."

"Allow me to express my own pleasure then, at being the sole black mark on your pristine record."

"I'm here to see if we can clean that up."

I gave the man an emphatic shake of my head. "Afraid I'll have to disappoint you and your electronic brains there again, Spartan. Nothing's changed. The answer's still the same."

"Nothing's changed *for you*. But the galaxy changes all around us, Buck."

"Okay. Enlighten me."

"Since we last talked, the SPARTAN-IV program's been a critical success. Commander Musa himself secured new funding for larger class sizes this time around."

"So you're launching a new recruiting drive."

"Soon, but I needed to finish up this one last bit of old business first." He reached over, picked up my bottle, and refilled my glass. "By which I mean you."

I waited for him to continue.

"As I recall, your main excuse for not joining the Spartans the last time we had this chat was that you didn't want to abandon your team. With our new class of Spartan-IVs, we have enough funding to widen our net."

"Wide enough to include . . . ?"

"Everyone on your team."

I gave him a look, and he jumped in to clarify.

"Specifically: Lance Corporal Kojo Agu, a.k.a. Romeo; Private First Class Michael Crespo, a.k.a. Mickey; and you."

"No room for Corporal Taylor Miles?"

"I'm assured that Dutch's commitment to the UNSC has reached an all-time low. Don't you think he'd be much happier reuniting with his wife?"

I knew he would, although that brought me straight up against the same question for myself. Veronica wasn't my wife, of course. She might never be. But I'd never loved anyone like I loved her.

I probably needed to tell her that. In person. Before I made a decision like this.

In my duller moments, I liked to ponder what a postwar life with her might look like. Apartment on Mars? Ranch on a resettled Draco III? Couple of kids?

Wonderful daydreams, to be sure. But she wasn't about to give up her job. She was doing too much good for too many people—often in ways I wasn't cleared to know about—and some days I liked to think I was doing the same.

One day, maybe, we'd try raising new lives rather than protecting the ones already here . . . but not today. And I was getting too far ahead of myself anyhow.

"Would you have considered the Rookie?" I asked in a hushed tone. "Not that it matters now, of course."

Jun frowned. "Yes. We would have had a space for him for sure."

I hoisted my glass toward the ex-Spartan, and he raised his as well. We clinked them together and drank.

"Does this mean you're in?" Jun said.

"Maybe."

"Well, that's an improvement over last time, at least."

THIRTEEN

I don't even know why we're talking about this," Veronica said to me a few weeks later—the fastest I could arrange for a mutual vacation. "You've already made up your mind." She walked out onto the balcony of our rented mountain chalet on Desdoron V, warming her hands around the mug of her hot toddy.

I followed straight after her like a dog on a proximity leash. "But that's the point," I said. "I don't want it to be just my decision. I want it to be *our* decision."

She didn't turn to look at me. Instead she gazed down at the lights of the little ski lodge nestled in the gentle valley at the bottom of the slope. I came up behind her and put my arms around her. She didn't elbow me in the ribs and knock me to the ground, which I took as a good sign.

"Why?" she said. "I don't have any say over what you do with your life."

"Yes," I said. "You do."

She tensed up at that. "You don't have any say over mine."

"No, I don't."

She relaxed into me and took a sip of her drink. "Well, that hardly seems fair."

"I thought we were talking about our relationship. I don't remember *fair* coming into it."

Now she elbowed me good for that one, but in a playful kind of way. With her ONI training, she could have killed me before I'd have even known it, so I took comfort in the fact I was still breathing.

"I love you, too," I said as I let her go and rubbed my ribs.

It was the first time I'd actually said those words to her, and I'd kinda backed my way into it. I waited to see if she'd freeze or run.

Or give me the greatest surprise.

Instead, her lips curled up into the cutest wry smirk. "So that's what this little vacation is really all about? It's more than just one last whoop-it-up before you dedicate your life to the Spartans?"

"You remember what you told me back in New Mombasa?"

She allowed herself a wistful smile. "I thought maybe you'd forgotten."

"Did you?"

She shook her head. "I said if you won the war, we'd talk about us."

I spread my arms wide. "Well, guess what? War's over."

She bobbed her head side to side in a way that said she might be willing to concede the point. The Covenant War had officially ended a year ago, but neither one of us had stopped fighting. The UNSC still hadn't run out of acceptable foes.

"So." Her voice rose in anticipation. "How do you want to play this?"

"That's really up to you," I said.

"Are you ready for this?" Veronica said.

I honestly wasn't sure what she meant. Were we talking about us or the SPARTAN-IV program? Veronica meant to have it both ways, and she wasn't about to tell me which topic we were discussing. Not yet.

ONI all the way.

I played along. "I think so."

"You'd better be more confident about it than that. Once you start down this road, there's no going back."

"I know that. It's a lifetime commitment." Whether marriage or becoming a Spartan, both held true. On the other hand, there's never been a need for an old-Spartans' home.

She looked me straight in the eyes. "It's a lot to think about."

I held steady, not wanting to get my hopes up. "That it is."

She took a long sip from her mug. Was she pondering or waiting? I let her savor her drink until I couldn't take the tension a moment longer.

"So what do you think?" I asked.

I've jumped into battle from orbit more times than I care to count. I've cracked open my coffin from inside and leaped straight into a firefight. I have saved worlds—or at least played my part in those rescues.

In all that time, I don't remember ever having my heart beat as fast as it was right then.

She pursed her lips at me as she considered the question.

Then she said: "You should do it."

I felt my blood pressure drop. She wanted me to join the Spartans. If she'd wanted for us to mutually resign and settle down somewhere into civilian life, she would have said *we*.

And maybe she would have said she loved me. Out loud.

I honestly didn't know how I felt about that. About the Spartan part, that is.

A part of me was disappointed, of course, but a huge chunk was relieved. Becoming a husband would have been a strange, new adventure into territory I didn't fully understand.

I already knew how to be a soldier.

Becoming a Spartan would take that to the next level, but

I'd be part of the same game, the one I'd been fighting my way through for my entire adult life. That took a bit of the sting out of it all. That and the fact that I'd be a superhuman: stronger, faster, sharper, better in almost every way.

Going in that direction would be irrevocable though. If the Spartans were going to invest that kind of money in me, they would—in a very real sense—own me. Or at least large parts of me that I wouldn't want to let get repossessed.

There was a third option, of course. We could get married anyhow, even if I became a Spartan. Veronica could keep doing her cloak-and-dagger stuff for ONI, and I could help save the galaxy in a less covert way. We'd just have rings on our fingers.

I could press her on that. We could try to have it both ways and see if we could make it work.

Once I thought about it a bit longer, though, I had to admit to myself—if not to Veronica—that I couldn't bear Option Three. For me, at least, it had to be one or the other: family or fighters.

Otherwise, I'd spend my entire second career as a Spartan worrying about my wife.

Being an ONI officer was the most dangerous job around. At least when I jumped out of dropships, I was outfitted as best as humanly possible. Veronica spent most of her days armored only by the shadows in which she could hide.

I already worried enough about losing her. There were times when we'd not been able to communicate with each other at all for weeks, and I'd start to wonder if I'd ever hear from her again. If I were lucky, someone in ONI would give me a heads-up and let me know if she was KIA, but I couldn't depend on that.

Instead, I'd had to learn to live with a kind of Schrödinger's fatalism, knowing that at any point she could be alive or dead. And I might never be able to find the damn box, much less open it.

If we married, I could only see that getting much, much worse.

I didn't realize that I'd gone silent until she cocked her head to one side to look up into my eyes. "You all right?" she said.

I gave her my best brave smile. "Never better."

"It's certainly not the end of us," she said. "You do realize that, right?"

"Of course."

She stepped closer and put her arms around me. "If I ever felt like I was ready to leave ONI," she said, "I'd leave it with you in a second."

I returned her embrace. "There's just too much going on right now."

"You don't know the half of it." She rested her head on my chest. "If you did, I'd have to kill you."

I chuckled at that. "The fact they keep making Spartans tells me enough."

"They made the right choice picking you. You'll be fantastic."

"So Jun keeps telling me."

She stepped back and looked up at me. "You're already the best man I know."

I put on a smile of false humility. "I owe it all to you."

She lowered her eyes then and blushed. I'd rarely seen her glow like that. "I do love you, you know."

I let out a deep sigh I didn't realize I'd been holding in, and a silly grin spread across my face. "Yeah, I do know. But it's great to hear it."

She reached out and took me by the hand, then turned and led me back into the warm comfort of the chalet. "If this is the last time we're going to see each other for a while, then we should make the most of every last moment."

And so we did. All week long.

FOURTEEN

L et me tell you a little bit now about how I actually became a Spartan.

This was now a month after Desdoron V. I spent a period of three weeks on Mars, in and out of surgeries and other so-called advanced therapies designed to transform me from a top-flight Helljumper into something approaching the closest thing humanity had to walking gods. And it hurt in every damn way it could.

When I say walking gods, I mean the Spartan-IIs. Like the old Greek Titans in the way that they live among us but are literally head and shoulders better in every way. And they're just about as hard to kill.

The fact we lost so many of them during the Covenant War tells you something about how horrific that conflict was.

The soldiers in the SPARTAN-III program were more like your standard gods of myth and legend, the Titans' kids. Hermes and Apollo and Aphrodite and such. If the Spartan-IIs are more powerful than you can imagine, Spartan-IIIs are probably just inside your limits.

The Spartan-IVs—my new designation—are like demigods then, the offspring of the real gods. Think Hercules. We can pass for regular people most of the time—something folks would generally have a hard time mistaking the earlier generations for—but inside, we're far more than that.

Or so I was told. Turns out to be mostly true. As I was going through the process, though, I was focused less on gods and more on devils.

That's what I called the doctors who worked on me, because it hurt like hell.

Ever seen an old house on Earth that's been gutted right to the studs and then refurbished from top to bottom? It looks mostly the same on the outside—maybe with a fresh coat of paint—but inside, it can be filled with cutting-edge class and gadgets that would make the original owners cry tears of sheer jealousy.

That's pretty much what they did to me.

They lengthened and augmented my bones to make them tougher than steel, which I needed, because they stretched and amped my muscles up so high I would have otherwise broken my own legs every time I jumped into the air. They replaced or reinforced every one of my joints to boot. By the end of it all, I was several centimeters taller than I'd been when I enlisted with the UNSC.

They super-myelinated my nervous system to amp up my reaction times. They improved my blood to make me immune to most toxins. They tell me I could eat a raw tree for dinner and get enough calories out of it to substitute for a six-course meal.

They souped up or replaced every one of my internal organs shy of my brain. I think. The SPARTAN-IV augmentation process is generally handled by ONI, after all, and you never know what those spooks might do. They don't seem to wrestle much with a lot of moral issues.

Case in point: They wired me up with enough onboard electronics that they'll have to recycle me rather than bury or burn me when I'm gone. I can see in the dark, interface with an AI, and I presume there's some kind of indestructible data recorder so they can monitor my health and performance.

I hear they make my MJOLNIR armor out of the same stuff.

By the time the docs were done, I felt a lot like my uncle Lou's fishing pole. In my mind, I was the same person, but I couldn't tell you how much of the original model was still there.

In the end, I suppose it didn't matter.

At one point, I asked one of the specialists, "What's all this junk do to my natural lifespan? Seeing as there's not that much natural about me anymore."

She cocked her head at me. "Honestly? We don't know. No Spartan has ever died of old age. If you're properly maintained and don't get killed, I suppose you could outlive most humans alive today."

"What's the record so far?"

She gave me a sympathetic shrug. "I can tell you that no Spartan has outlived the average human lifespan yet."

That confused me for a moment. Then I got it. "Oh."

I didn't see too much of Mickey and Romeo. The docs wanted us to focus on the changes in our own bodies rather than comparing notes with our pals. Since we were all unique adults, coming into the program at varying ages and with different skills, the docs had to tailor our treatments specifically to each of us. We were battle-hardened vets, not soft, malleable kids that could be cookie-cuttered into Spartans.

When I did run into the two of them, we traded jokes about how much it hurt and what whiners we all were.

"Never thought turning into an invulnerable superhero would ache so damn much," Mickey said. Despite the dark circles under his eyes, he looked happier than he'd been since the Rookie got killed. He and Romeo had come to some kind of détente over that, mostly by refusing to talk or even think about it.

"At least we'll have plenty of new scars to show the ladies." Romeo flashed a grin at one of the doctors as she walked by. It heartened me to know that not that much about him—about who he really was inside—had changed.

We weren't the only ones getting the full SPARTAN workover at the time. There were a good dozen or two of us there at any given point. We hailed from all walks of the UEG. Human men and women of all races, from colonies of all sizes. The only things we had in common were our total commitment to the UNSC— and our humanity.

In my spare moments, I hit it off with a guy named Hideo Wakahisa, a young guy who'd hailed from Newsaka, a distant colony that lay just beyond Draco III. As a kid, he'd visited New Albany with his mother on business, and he'd fallen in love with the place. We had that in common at least, which gave us an edge over most of the other people there, who could only bond over their days in the UNSC.

He was tall enough as a Helljumper that I could have mistaken him for a Spartan before the transformation, except he was far too lanky. When the docs were through with him, he towered over me, and I'd grown an aching, fair bit myself.

Despite all the pain, I had never felt better in my entire life. My body became stronger and more resilient. My senses sharpened so much I could read the fine print on the bottom of the releases they made me sign, even from across the room. I could hear nurses coming from several rooms away.

It took some getting used to, but I gotta admit, I really liked it.

Veronica came to visit me at the Mars base while I was in my final round of recovery—just before I shipped out for training— and she tried to reassure me about my concerns regarding mortality as we relaxed in my private quarters. I was used to bunking on warships, and by comparison, my three rooms and a private shower seemed luxurious. In my rebuilt body, though, it somehow felt cramped, like I might accidentally knock a hole in a wall every time I turned around, and she sensed my unease.

"You're not already thinking about retirement, are you?" she joked with a wry smile. "Just focus on the job, and you'll do fine. Distractions like that can get your head shot off."

"Just wondering if I might someday start wearing out like an old warship."

"It's not like you run on batteries. And even if you did, we'd just replace them."

"Might be cheaper to just replace me with a brand-new Spartan at that point. Once a ship's too old to be any use on the battlefield, they sell it for scrap."

She punched me in the shoulder, and I pretended like it hurt. The docs had treated me like I was made of glass during the entire enhancement procedure, and that was the first time anyone had done anything aggressive toward me. I barely felt it.

Then she caressed my arm where she'd hit me, and that felt just as good as it always had. "Don't tempt me," she said.

I allowed myself a smile. That seemed to work fine, too.

"So, I assume you came by to kick my tires and see if the chassis can still handle you?"

She raised her hand to punch me again, and I flinched so hard she couldn't help laughing at me. "Maybe some other time," she said. "When you're fully healed and the docs have signed off on you. I wouldn't want to break you."

"Likewise."

She hesitated, and I realized she had something more to say. I put a gentle hand on hers. "I take it this isn't just a social call."

"I wanted to see you."

"Go ahead," I said. "You can't break my heart. Not after what the docs did to it. Just—let me down gently."

She rolled her eyes at me, but in a loving way. "I'm going to talk to the doctors about adjusting your meds. They need to cut down on whatever goofy-juice they're feeding you."

I grinned at her. "I'm sorry. I just can't help it. I feel so—"

I rolled my hands around in front of me as I grasped for the right word.

"Stupid?" Veronica offered.

I ignored her jibe. "Alive! Like everything's more real than before. It's all so sharp, I'm surprised it doesn't slice me open—except that I'm so tough now I don't know what could get through my skin."

Veronica fidgeted in her chair. "That's wonderful—for you. But like I said, I'm not here on a social call."

"I'm not even fully finished with recovery yet. I thought maybe we'd have a little time for some R&R before I had to report for training."

"The Spartans don't mess around," she said. "And you all heal damn fast. By the time you're ready to handle me, they'll send you straight off to training camp."

"Spoilsport."

"You volunteered for this big metamorphosis."

"And yet, for the things that really matter, nothing's changed at all. What do you need?"

The amusement faded from her face. "It's nothing official yet, but our spies among the Front hear that there may be a mole among the most recent class of Spartans.

"What?" I had a hard time imagining anyone going through all of this with the intention of turning on the UNSC the moment it was finished.

"Listen to me. One of the new Spartans may secretly be a member of the Front." She shrugged.

Up until that point, I thought maybe she'd been joking with me because I was still healing up. "You're kidding. What the hell am I saying? Of course you're not kidding. And you have no idea who?"

"We're pretty sure it's not you."

"Great news. At least that narrows it down a bit."

"And I vouched for Romeo and Mickey, too."

"Aha. And you're sure about them, too?" I joked.

"It could be just about anyone else. Every member of this class passed a thorough background check and psych evaluation, and we're going through communications records and lists of past associations. So far, nothing firm has turned up, but it might just mean the mole's buried that deep."

"So how do you know there's a traitor?"

"We picked up some Front chatter with them effectively howling with glee about getting one of their own into the program."

"And you haven't been able to track down who they meant?"

"These things take time."

"And you don't have enough of it."

"Not at the moment. Not only do we not know who the traitor is, but we also don't know when or where they'll strike. Hell, we're not even sure the Front's not just playing with us to get us to waste our resources chasing ghosts."

"Assuming they're not, you think this mole will go after the SPARTAN program?"

Veronica frowned. "It's one thing for the Front to wind up with a Spartan of its own. It would be an entirely new level of bad for them to compromise the program."

"But we can't depend on whoever it is outing themselves that way. They might just lay low until training is over."

"It all depends on how patient they—or the Front leadership, such as it is—want to be."

I rubbed my eyes. "You don't think this has anything to do with the revolt we stopped on Draco III, do you?"

She shook her head. "This infiltration attempt has been in the works for a long time. Despite the fact the United Rebel Front has the word "united" right in its name, they're really only that together with respect to their ideals, and just barely. They rarely show such a level of coordination."

I thought about this for a moment. "Doesn't ONI have some kind of fail-safe on people like me?"

"You mean a kill switch we can use to disable you by remote?"

I nodded, not sure I wanted to hear an honest answer.

"While I'm sure someone above me would love to have that option on hand, it doesn't exist. It's just too much of a security risk. If there was a way to just shut a Spartan down, it might fall into the wrong hands."

"So you just trust us?"

"Given that we're talking about ONI, 'trust' probably isn't the right word, but okay, sure. Spartans find themselves in all sorts of insane situations. We don't see the wisdom in building any kind of artificial limits. Spartans need every edge they can get."

"Right up until one of them betrays us all, or so you say."

"That's where Alpha-Nine comes in." She still called us by our old squad name even though we officially were no longer part of the Corps. That was fine by me. I didn't have any plans to retire it. "You and Romeo and Mickey have an impeccable reputation. After the work you did in New Mombasa, I'm telling you that *no one* at ONI questions your loyalty. Just about everyone else, though, is under suspicion."

I blew out a long breath. "You can't narrow it down any

further? We have to investigate everyone else in the program one by one?"

"If it was as simple as lining them all up and interrogating them, believe me, we'd do that," Veronica said. "ONI has no qualms about locking people up and asking them lots of questions. But that's not likely to work here."

"You spooks don't know how to ask the right questions anymore?"

"Back during the war, the sides were a lot clearer. Now that we're fighting other humans again as well, things get muddy real fast. Many soldiers who were fantastic against the Covenant have now balked at battling the Front or any of the other dozens of homegrown terrorist groups across our worlds."

"That sounds like any of us might fit the bill. So how do you know that doesn't include me? Obviously, proving myself against the Covenant doesn't mean anything. You just said so."

Veronica winced at that. "True, but when you and I became involved . . ."

She let my imagination fill in the rest.

"Seriously?" I held my head in both hands. I gave thanks that the docs had reinforced my skull, otherwise, my brain felt like it might have burst out of it. "Wow. ONI knows about us—and they're treating me like they were your dad."

"My dad's dead."

"Dammit, you know what I mean."

She put a hand on my shoulder. "Buck. After New Mombasa, ONI put you through the same kind of investigation they do with their own agents. You passed with flying colors. The whole team did. *That's* why I've been able to use Alpha-Nine when it's mattered over the years."

I considered yelling about it, getting upset, and carrying on. I don't know who would have blamed me. After all, when you start a relationship with someone, you like to think it's not with the entire organization they work for.

On the other hand, it wasn't like I didn't know who Veronica was. I had long suspected something like this, but we'd always danced around the subject. Now the music had finally ended.

"I, ah, suppose that's good news." I took my hands off my head and held her hands instead.

Her fingers looked smaller than ever. I was several centimeters taller and twenty kilos heavier than I'd been before, and Veronica seemed tiny now. I'd never thought of her as fragile, but compared to the new me, I suppose she was. The doctors had really worked over every centimeter of me.

"Of course it is." She smiled up at me, relieved.

She stood up and stroked my forehead as she gazed into my eyes. Then she gave me a long, loving kiss.

"Just get through your training, Buck, and keep your eyes open. I don't know if they'll make a move now or wait till later, but you're in a unique position to get to know the rest of your class far better than any ONI agent could."

"I'll do my duty and spy on my fellow Spartans. For justice."

She gave me a smile. "As for that R&R, I already have us booked for a week at a resort in Acidalia when your training's through."

"You know just what to say to cheer me up."

In that regard, I would soon find that Captain O'Day was the direct opposite of Veronica Dare.

ammit, Gunny!" Captain O'Day shouted in my face. "Spartans don't cry!"

"I ain't crying, Captain," I said as I winced again in agony. "I just got some nanotech in my eye."

There was more than a bit of truth in what she said. I'll admit that I had something salty flowing out of my eyes, but it had more to do with the fact that I couldn't stop the pain. The medical alterations had sent my hormones into a crazed spiral. I hadn't felt this raw and vulnerable since I'd hit puberty.

When the docs had certified me fit for release, I could have whooped with joy. I'd been cooped up for weeks and couldn't wait to take my new bones out for a spin. If I'd known what lay waiting for me in the secret SPARTAN training camp facility orbiting a barely remembered dwarf planet, I'd have whimpered for mercy instead.

It had been over twenty-five years since I'd been through basic training, and since then I'd worked my way up to the rank of gunnery sergeant and become an ONI on-demand soldier with my own fireteam under my command. I wasn't used to having someone else not only tell me what to do on the field of battle, but holler that I was doing it wrong, too.

The worst part is that Captain O'Day was right. I'd built up all sorts of bad habits over the years, and layered in lots of different excuses for that behavior to quiet any qualms I might have had about it. Now O'Day and the rest of the ONI trainers stripped all those excuses away and made me feel about as sharp and experienced as a six-year-old child.

Which is the age at which they allegedly started out the Master Chief, I guess, but that's not my point.

When it came to discipline, I'd gotten sloppy. Thankfully, Captain O'Day wasn't having any of that. She stood a quarter meter shorter than me, but she was sharp and lean as a stiletto. Any one of us could have torn her to pieces without breaking a sweat if so inclined, but she was such a fierce force of determination and will that none of us would have dared try.

She was committed to whipping me and the rest of my Spartan class into shape, whether we were ready for it or not. With a face as angular and unassuming as a hatchet, she glared into my watery eyes and gave it to me straight. "The United Nations Space Command did not just transform you worthless sacks of shit into the finest fighting men and women the galaxy has to offer *just to have you collapse there and whine about it!*"

"I think they chose poorly," Romeo muttered. He'd fallen to a knee, supposedly to check on me. "But don't think I'm above taking advantage of it."

O'Day lanced him with a glare that could have stripped off the paint still left on Romeo's armor. If he'd had even a bit of shame in him.

"Tell her she can have it all back, Gunny," Mickey said much more quietly as he leaned against a nearby wall, gasping for air. "Just as long as we don't have to go through that again."

"That" in this case was a combat training mission held in the space station's largest war games chamber, which was saying something, considering the entire place was the size of a sprawling starship. I'd played football on smaller fields.

That day's exercise pitted us against an endless onslaught of the best automated weaponry ONI's black budget could buy, guided by a dozen of the UNSC's sharpest combat veterans. They used non-lethal rounds, which I'm sure they only downgraded to so they could protect their investments in us, but they didn't hold back in any other way. Every one of us fresh Spartans had taken several slugs in uncomfortable spots. Fake or not, the damn things hurt.

I'd decided to make the most of the elaborate terrain they'd mocked up for the place, which was apparently generated by fancy holographics and risers. The environment was startlingly life-like, including not only a lush jungle above, but also a warren of twisting and turning tunnels below. Many of the tunnels cut low enough that you had to crawl through them, but they'd included a number of taller areas where you could sit or even stand if you needed a breather.

The best part about the tunnels was they didn't have any cameras on them. When the chamber had been carved out of the station, they'd installed cameras in the walls and ceiling, but they didn't have any pointing down below. That supposedly gave us a sporting chance to be able to sneak around and slip up behind our automated foes, but I sometimes just went that way so I could rest my aching, elongated bones.

At one point during that day's exercise, I moved out of what I had thought was an excellent hiding spot and stumbled straight across an automatic shotgun I could have sworn hadn't been there before. Damn thing spat non-lethal—but extremely painful— buckshot right into my chest.

None of it pierced my armor, but the blast knocked me back

off my feet and bruised my ribs. It felt like a Hunter had been stomping up and down on my chest, trying to squeeze my heart out through my mouth. For a long moment, I couldn't breathe, and I briefly wondered if, despite Veronica's assertions, the doctors hadn't somehow installed a buckshot-activated kill-switch under my solar plexus.

"This isn't fair," said Kovsky, one of our fellow fresh faces, an ink-skinned woman with stubby black braids framing her wide, angry eyes. "You send us into this hellhole of a training camp, outnumbered and outgunned, without even our Mjolnir armor?"

O'Day marched straight up to Kovsky and kicked her in the crotch. I realize it's not the same for women as it is for men, but poor Kovsky folded over like someone had cut her in half.

"You think we just hand you that armor?" O'Day hissed. "You have to *earn those rags*!"

"Yeah, but haven't we already done that?" Schein said, his pale, stubbly face glistening with an unhealthy sweat. "We got admitted to the program. We went through the procedures. We're already Spartans, Captain."

One look at O'Day told me that Schein was either the bravest or the dumbest man I'd ever known. The two things weren't mutually exclusive. He had to know he was going to piss off the captain, though, and he looked ready to protect his nether regions, at least, if it came to that.

"You are Spartans when you graduate this program," she said in a way that sounded like she was stomping the ground for emphasis with every word, even though her legs never twitched a centimeter. "And you graduate this program when *I* say so. Do you know what that means?"

Schein glanced around at the rest of us as if asking for help. No one seemed ready to step between him and the captain. I might have considered if I hadn't still been too busy wondering if I would ever be able to fill my lungs with sweet, sweet air again.

Schein just shook his head.

O'Day snarled at him. "It means you're not a goddamn Spartan until *I* say you're a goddamn Spartan! You might feel like a super-hero, but right now you're as useless as a baby—and the *UNSC doesn't need any goddamn babies!*"

I fought the temptation to beg for a bottle and struggled to my feet instead. "Yes, sir, Captain, sir!" I said, as well as my lungs would allow.

Some of the others in our training class of twenty might have thought I was just sucking up to Captain O'Day, but the fact was I knew she was right. We all did. That's what was really killing us.

"You see?" O'Day clapped me on the back. "Now *that's* the kind of attitude I want! Get shot in the chest? Get your sorry ass back up and get moving. No screwing around. No self-pity, no jealousy, no wondering why you don't have a proper Mjolnir set of rags yet. Just get your lazy ass up and go!"

She laughed at me then. "Of course, Gunny, *you* probably would have an even better attitude if you could keep from walking right into a shotgun blast like that, huh?"

I didn't say a word. I just headed straight back for the starting gate of the training run. Jawing with the captain about my supposed credentials or my relative lack of happiness wasn't going to make the day go any faster. Just get through this damn thing without getting shot. Again.

I couldn't tell you know many times we charged through the run. I only know that, in the end, we finally made it.

I cried all the way to the infirmary, but they were tears of joy. That didn't last long though.

I would have gone straight to my quarters rather than bother the medics about some bruised ribs that now hurt a good deal less than my wounded ego. But Captain O'Day had insisted that I follow regulations and get checked out. "We've put a lot of effort into you, Buck," the captain said. "You may have only scratched your paint, but the docs deserve their chance to buff it out."

With my Spartan blood working overtime, I was feeling pretty good within the hour. I was just about to leave, when they hauled in Wakahisa, my old pal from the transformation facility on Mars—or what was left of him.

The medics wheeled the kid in on an extra-long gurney that was covered with a white sheet, but the blood underneath it had already seeped through in several spots. One end was soaked crimson, and when a doc raced up and drew the sheet back, I saw why.

Wakahisa's head had been all but torn from his body, and his amped-up arteries had bled out like a fire hose. His eyes hung open and lifeless, the whites shining through all the rest of that red.

"What the hell happened to him?" I said, sitting up in shock. I'd sat next to the kid at breakfast just that morning, shooting the shit about our neighboring home colonies. He was a lousy card player but a damn fine young soldier. In a lot of ways, he reminded me of the Rookie when he'd started out with Alpha-Nine. All raw talent with not nearly enough sense running through it—yet.

Now he'd never get the chance to use those talents, or all those Spartan enhancements ONI had engineered in him.

The doc who'd drawn back the sheet let it fall back down over Wakahisa's face, and then reeled away in dismay and disgust. And this was one of the people who'd torn me apart and put me back together better than ever. She'd probably done the same for the dead man, and seeing him like that was more than she could bear.

I slipped out of my bed, yanking off the various feeds and lines running into me. The doc didn't react at all. "Hey! What *happened*?" I asked.

"Found him out there in the training chamber like that," one of the medics said. He sounded distant and vacant, still absorbing the horror of it all.

"He didn't return from the field when the call went out," said the other. "We couldn't raise him on the comm. Commander Musa sent us out to find him."

I looked to the doc. "Someone blocked all those electronic locators you stuck in us?"

The doc recovered a bit and shook her head. "No. Someone *tore* them out." She pointed toward the blood-soaked end of the sheet covering Wakahisa. "They're mostly up under the jaw, the ones that aren't directly integrated into the armor."

"Who did this?" I asked.

"We didn't see anyone else out there," the first medic said. "Whoever did this was long gone by the time we got there. It could have been anyone."

"Sure," I said. "Anyone who could overpower a combat-trained Spartan and rip his throat out."

Other than Captain O'Day, the only other people who'd been out there in the training chamber during the exercise had been Spartans. Hard as it was to believe, the killer had to be a Spartan, too.

Why did Veronica always have to be so right?

Commander Musa's voice rumbled over the station's PA system then: "Attention all personnel. We have had an unfortunate incident during today's combat training exercise. As a result of this, all junior personnel are ordered to return to their quarters immediately. You are hereby confined to your quarters until further notice."

When it came to Spartans, I figured there weren't many more junior than me. "Am I free to go yet, doc?"

She came over and put a gentle hand on my arm. "You checked out fine. You should be all right by now. Just get to your quarters as fast as you can."

Although I wanted to run right down to the rec room— where most of the uninjured Spartans would have gone after our training—and interrogate everyone I could find, the doctor was right. I was no cop. If I ignored orders and did something that rash, I'd just muddle up the evidence, and the last thing Commander Musa or Captain O'Day needed was a bunch of charged-up Spartans trampling every bit of evidence around them—including maybe each other.

I made my way back to the barracks and to the cramped quarters I shared with the rest of Alpha-Nine. Romeo and Mickey had beaten me there and were sitting on their bunks, which—along with mine—framed the small room's walls. They'd busted out a deck of cards and were playing poker on top of Mickey's footlocker, which they'd hauled into the center of our small patch of floor.

"Deal you in?" Romeo said with a hungry grin.

"Careful, Gunny," Mickey said. "He's about to clean me out."

"Consider it yet another gentle lesson in why you're such an awful player," Romeo said to him.

"What's that supposed to mean?"

"You don't really want to know."

I shook my head at them and long-stepped over the footlocker to reach my bunk, opposite the door. "Romeo's already taught me that lesson."

Mickey squinted at me. "You know something."

Romeo cocked his head my way. "This isn't just a drill?"

I frowned. "You ever know Musa to just yank your chain for fun?"

"We haven't been here all that long."

"Captain O'Day might try something like that," I said. "Not the commander. He's a straight shooter."

Mickey nodded. "Those Spartan-IIs don't mess around."

"Can you really call him a Spartan if he never wore the armor?" said Romeo.

"It's not his fault his body rejected the transformation treatments," I said. "Even in that wheelchair of his, I bet he could take you apart."

"I can't even imagine that," said Mickey. "Get abducted by ONI at six years old and have a doomed-to-die clone put in your place—and *then* you get crippled long before you're even the right size for the armor? Tragic, man."

"Ah, that's all bullshit," Romeo said. "All that 'kidnapped and cloned' crap. You really will believe what anyone tells you, won't you?"

Mickey shrugged off Romeo's doubts.

"At least he didn't wind up dead like some of the others in his SPARTAN class," I said.

Mickey tossed in his cards. "Without him, there wouldn't be a SPARTAN-IV program at all."

As the Covenant War came to an end, Musa had seen the chance to restart the SPARTAN program, but to recruit volunteers from the ranks of the UNSC rather than plucking them out of their cribs, thin air, or wherever. It worked better than anyone—outside of maybe Musa himself—could have hoped.

He'd patterned the new program on the original SPARTAN-I program from back before the turn of the century, which had taken top soldiers and improved upon them as best they could with the technology of the day. They'd called it ORION back then, but when they rebooted the program for another shot, they changed the name and came up with SPARTAN-II instead.

That's military logic for you. The original program had failed because it proved too costly for what the UNSC got out of it—even though I hear one of those first recruits was none other than Sergeant Johnson. They renamed it in order to distance themselves, but they retain the numbers to show the sequence. ORION as SPARTAN-I to spackle over it.

Anyhow, word was that Musa had used the incredible success of the first class of Spartan-IVs to divorce the program from the Navy and, more specifically, Naval Intelligence. While the SPARTAN program worked in concert with both of those groups—and recruited heavily from them—the Spartans became their own branch of the UNSC's military. That gave them a lot more leeway with their missions, and it meant they weren't under anyone's thumb.

Honestly, that was one of the selling points for me. Working with ONI too long makes a soldier feel dirty. Much as I love Veronica, I was happy to wash my hands of that.

"What's up, Gunny?" Mickey said. "Give it to us straight."

I just spat it out. "Spartan Wakahisa got killed during the exercise today."

Mickey paled, but Romeo just laughed. "I thought you were the one who caught the most buckshot," he said.

"No, I mean killed dead," I said. "Murdered actually."

"Bullshit," said Mickey.

"I was in the infirmary when they brought him in."

Romeo threw in his cards, too. "What happened?"

I shrugged. "I wasn't there. But whoever killed him ripped out his tracker implant."

Romeo made a face. "Right out of his neck?"

I gave him a nod and then froze. Romeo and Mickey spotted that straightaway and spun around to see what had caught my attention.

Jun had appeared in our door. He looked as grim as an undertaker. "Gentlemen."

We leaped to our feet and saluted. He responded in kind and then stepped aside.

"At ease," said a voice just down the hall. An instant later, Commander Musa rolled through our door. Jun stepped up behind him and stood in the doorway once again.

"Spartans," Musa said. "We have a situation."

"How's that, sir?" I said. Romeo and Mickey might have been the same rank as me now, but they deferred to me out of habit.

"Buck. I assume you've told Agu and Crespo what you witnessed in the infirmary."

"Yes, sir. I hadn't given them much in the way of details yet though."

"Do you *have* much in the way of details?"

I frowned. "No, sir."

"Then allow me to fill you in." He glanced at the others, and we all gave him the go-ahead to continue.

"Spartan Wakahisa was murdered in the combat training chamber during today's exercise. He was found in one of the tunnels. It seems the killer forcibly removed some of the circuitry under Wakahisa's jaw to prevent our systems from being alerted to his status.

"We knew instantly that something had gone wrong, of course, but not the extent of it. When Wakahisa didn't report in after the end of the training exercise, Jun here went looking for him."

Jun then took over. "I found him lying in the section of the tunnels farthest from the entrance. His body was still warm. I called in our medical team to remove him while I scoured the area for evidence. I also had our admin team scan the recordings of the training. By that, we were able to eliminate a number of Spartan trainees from suspicion."

"You really think a Spartan would do something like this?" Mickey said.

Jun ignored the question. "The trainees who didn't go down into the tunnels—or who emerged from them before Wakahisa went down into the tunnels—were eliminated. That leaves us with a short list of possible suspects."

I felt a chill run through me as Jun gave us each a meaningful glance. I'd been down in the tunnels for a good part of the exercise.

"That list includes every Spartan in this room," Jun said.

"We didn't have anything to do with it," I said.

"And you can speak for your two friends here?" Musa said.

"They can pipe up for themselves," I said. "But I've worked with them for years now, and I've trusted them with my life on every operation. They've never let me down."

"I didn't even see Wakahisa," Romeo said. "Not since the start of the exercise."

Mickey shook his head in agreement. "I had no idea. None at all. I was too busy trying to not get shot myself."

Jun reached into the breast pocket of his jacket then and pulled out a sealed plastic bag about the size of a fist. A broken chain and a circular medallion sat inside of it, and they were smeared with blood.

Even painted red as it was, I recognized the medallion instantly. It had been molded to resemble the surface of the Moon.

It belonged to Mickey.

"We found this clutched in Wakahisa's hand," Jun said. He kept any hint of accusation out of his tone, but we all knew what it meant.

Mickey's eyes grew wide as the barrel of a grenade launcher. "That's mine," he said in a hollow voice. He glanced at me for support. "The Rookie and I bought them after the end of the war. Something to remember our common home. He lost most of his family there during the Battle for Earth."

"And you?" asked Musa.

"I'm an orphan." He swallowed hard. "Lived in foster homes most of my life."

"Shuffled around a lot?"

He nodded. "Joined the UNSC the day I turned eighteen."

"That's mandatory for all wards of the state."

"I'd have signed up either way."

"I'm glad to hear that," Musa said. "Especially given how your parents died."

Mickey flushed red, and I put a hand on his arm to make sure he wouldn't launch himself at our commander. Mickey was as stable a guy as anyone I'd served with, but his family history tended to be a raw nerve.

"That's not fair, sir," I said to Musa. "Spartan Crespo has an exemplary record, and you cannot judge him by the actions of his parents."

"What the hell is he babbling about?" Romeo batted Mickey in the chest with the back of his hand. "Your parents died in an accident."

Mickey's jaw bulged so hard from biting back his anger I thought the joints might crack.

"That's not a lie," Musa said. "But it's not the entire truth either."

"What?" Romeo wasn't going to let this go.

Mickey spoke in a hoarse whisper. "They were part of the insurrection on Luna. They were trying to bomb a building."

"Oh shit."

Had there been space in the room, Romeo would have backed away. As it was, he could only squirm in his boots.

"What's that got to do with today?" I said to Commander Musa. He held up Mickey's medallion.

"I haven't worn that since I became a Spartan," Mickey said. "It doesn't fit around my neck anymore."

"So how did it get into the training chamber?" asked Jun.

Mickey shrugged. "It should be in my footlocker."

Romeo groaned. "Which he never locks."

"I don't own anything worth stealing." Mickey glanced at the bloody medallion. "At least, that's what I thought."

"Someone must have taken it and planted it on Wakahisa," I said.

"Who would want to frame Mickey?" Romeo said.

The man shook his head in disbelief.

"When was the last time you saw it?" Jun said to Mickey.

"This morning," he said. "I hung it on the inside of my footlocker's lid so I could see it every time I opened it."

Musa craned his neck around to speak to Jun. "Pull the records for the hallway cameras here for the past eight hours, as well as the movement logs for any of the trainees on the possible suspects list. If that doesn't come up with any hits, widen that to cover the rest of the occupants of the station."

"Right away, sir."

He looked back at the three of us. "You'd better hope we find something, or we're going to look at each of you under a microscope."

Romeo shrugged his broadened shoulders. "I don't know if I'd fit under a microscope anymore, sir."

Musa arched an eyebrow at him. "Not in one piece, you won't."

Romeo shut his lips tight and gave Commander Musa a nod to acknowledge the seriousness of the situation.

Musa wheeled himself out of the room to continue the investigation of Wakahisa's death on other fronts. Jun assigned us temporary quarters at the other end of the hall. "You're all off duty until further notice. Stay in there, and don't leave until I come for you," he said. "I'll have your meals brought in to you."

"Are we under arrest?" Mickey asked. He was taking getting framed personally, and I didn't see how I could blame him for it.

"Not at all," Jun said. "But we'll find it easier to catch whoever did this if you're out of the way."

"Maybe that's just what this asshole who took Mickey's medallion wants," said Romeo.

"Maybe," said Jun, "but it's what Commander Musa wants, too. So keep your heads down and your noses clean. I'll come check on you shortly."

Meaning "whenever I get around to it."

As much as I respected Musa and knew he was right about keeping us out of the way, it grated on me to have to be put in a cooler like that. Mickey lay on his bed in shock, staring at the ceiling, not doing or saying anything, while Romeo paced back and forth in what little room we had.

I couldn't take the silence. "Do you have any idea who might have done this?" I asked Mickey.

He didn't say anything.

"Mickey?"

Nothing.

"Spartan Crespo!"

"I don't know," he said in a not terribly convincing way. "But I think it might have been Schein."

Romeo scoffed. "That idiot? Do you know how much money I've taken off him since we got here? Can't bluff for shit."

"He's a lot more serious about his politics than his cards," Mickey said.

"What are you getting at?" I asked.

Mickey gave me a pained frown. "It's not the things he said to me so much as how he said them. Nothing seditious, but with what happened to my parents, I'm a little, you know—"

"Sensitive?" I said.

"Yeah."

"Maybe that's just the way he talks," Romeo said. "I mean, he *is* an idiot."

Mickey sucked at his teeth. "And he saw me looking at my medallion once. Commented on it."

"Ah," I said. "You should say something to Jun or Commander Musa about it."

"You think?"

I tried to raise Jun on the comm system, but he didn't answer me. That's when we heard the first shots fired.

Jun's order to stay put lost a lot of its weight. Mickey and Romeo glanced at me for my lead, and I gave the door a sharp nod.

We charged down the brightly lit hall that ran through the barracks part of the space station, ducking past the other Spartans sticking their heads out through their doors to see what was going on. I doubt if most of them were still confined to quarters as well. After a long day's training, they were taking a well-earned break that had just been ruined.

Some of them shouted at us to ask what was going on. Others leaped into action right behind us, racing toward the direction from which the shots had come.

The rec room sat at the end of the hall, but we never got that far. Before we reached it, Captain O'Day came heading our way at top speed.

"Get back!" she shouted at us. *"Now!"*

I hesitated for an instant in confusion. My training told me to obey a superior officer's orders, but my first instinct was to ignore her and keep heading for the danger instead.

That's when the hallway behind O'Day exploded. A fireball chased down the hall after her and flung her toward us.

Gravity cut out at the same time as the explosion, and that threw me off. I wanted to try to catch O'Day, but I found I couldn't brace myself properly for it. And then the shock wave from the blast sent me, Mickey, and Romeo flying backward, spinning into the other Spartans charging up behind us.

It was all I could do to cover my head and hope for luck to shine on me one more time. The force of the explosion battered all of us, sending us skittering off the walls, floor, and ceiling, not to mention each other. We wound up in a heap of tangled and bruised limbs at the far end of the hallway.

The fireball petered out before it reached most of us, but the edge of it caught the captain, setting her legs on fire. With my ears ringing from the blast, I shoved myself toward her and patted her down with my bare hands until the flames went out. She'd been knocked senseless and didn't bat an eye through the whole thing.

Alarms blared throughout the station. I shoved myself out of the pile of people and tried to get a better look at Captain O'Day.

Mickey grabbed my shoulder. "We need to get her out of here!" he said.

I was reluctant to move her much for fear that she'd been se-verely injured, but we couldn't leave her floating there scorched like that either. I scooped her up as gently as I could, relying on my zero-G training to keep me from banging her around too much.

"Clear a way for me," I said.

That's when the massive viewport in the rec room gave way. It seemed like a miracle that it hadn't happened at the same time as the blast, but the SPARTAN program likes to build things to last. In this case, they lasted about thirty seconds more than I would have guessed.

The viewport looked out from the rec room into the airless space through which the space station swung on its orbit around its dark dwarf planet. When it gave way, the room decompressed violently. Anyone and anything in the room at the time got sucked straight out into the raw vacuum, which tugged at every exposed part of the station.

The air in the hallway became a howling wind, pulling us toward the rec room as if a giant were sucking us through a straw. I tried to maintain my hold on Captain O'Day, but she got snagged on something and was wrenched out of my grasp.

Struggling to hold on to her cost me my best chance at finding a grip that could stop me from heading toward the rec room. I glanced off three different doorways, getting pulled closer to the end of the hall, beyond which lay certain death.

Just in time, the emergency shutter slammed closed, sealing us off from the damaged room. That didn't stop my momentum, though, and I smacked into it hard. If I hadn't been a Spartan, the impact might have splattered me as if I'd leaped off a skyscraper. It still hurt like hell, but my reinforced bones kept me from becoming a pancake.

And then Captain O'Day—who must have torn free from whatever she'd been caught on—landed on me. I saw her coming at me, and I did my best to cushion her. Because she'd passed out, though, she had no means of helping herself. Little did I realize that she landed at a terrible angle, and died instantly.

The rest of the Spartans in the hallway had managed to find themselves a handhold, so no one else landed on me. Their belongings hailed down upon me, though, battering me like a storm of rocks. I tried to shield O'Day with my body as best I could, huddling over her and turning my back to the incoming objects to let them bounce off me.

I didn't know I was already too late to do her any good.

When I turned back around, I spotted Romeo and Mickey hauling themselves toward me, hand over hand. At some point, the lights in the hallway had all gone red. Commander Musa's voice sounded over the public comm system: "We have experienced a catastrophic breach! All personnel are to remain in their quarters!"

"That's where we screwed it up," Romeo said. "Shoulda followed orders."

"We weren't the only ones," Mickey said, pointing toward the other trainees pulling themselves back into their quarters. "Not by far."

"None of them wound up with every loose thing in the hall slamming down on them though," I said as I examined O'Day's body and finally saw she was already gone. "Dammit."

I scooped her up with one arm and glared at Romeo and Mickey, daring them to tell me to leave her behind. I tried to head back to our quarters, only to find we'd been sealed off from them too, so we holed up inside an empty room instead.

The gravity came back an hour later. Commander Musa warned us before he had it activated, which gave us a chance to slip into our borrowed room's bunks and avoid a repeat of the incident in the hallway. Soon afterward, he appeared on the viewscreen built into the back of our room's door, looking like someone had shot him in the gut.

"You are to return to your proper quarters, Spartans."

"Sir," I said. "Captain O'Day—"

"We're aware of her status, Buck." He lowered his eyes for a moment. "Leave her in one of the bunks there. A crew will come by to take care of her remains shortly. We still have a lot of work to do for the living before we can take care of our dead."

"Can I ask what happened, sir?"

Romeo and Mickey had been swapping speculations about the explosion the entire time, right up until I told them to shut their yaps for a bit. The ridiculous notion of a Covenant fighter entering slipspace right outside the rec room finally broke it for me.

Musa sighed and gestured to shut off the viewscreen. Just as he did, Mickey piped up. "Sir! I'd like to know if I'm still a suspect."

The screen went dark. I gave Mickey a sympathetic clap on the shoulder as he and Romeo left the room. Before I followed them, I stopped for a moment to pay my respects to Captain O'Day. She'd pushed me as hard as any drill sergeant, and I'd never had a chance to thank her for that.

When we got back to our regular quarters, no one felt much like talking. Mickey shoved his footlocker back under his bunk, and we threw ourselves down on our mattresses to be alone with our thoughts. Or as alone as you can get in a UNSC barracks, at least.

The viewscreen on the inside of our quarters' door lit up a moment later. "I'm sorry, Spartan Crespo," Musa said. "It's been a terrible day, but you, of all people, deserve to know."

He took a moment to compose himself. "Checking the records, we discovered that another Spartan had slipped into your quarters this morning before the training exercise began. When Jun, O'Day, and I went to confront him, we found him waiting for us in the rec room. He threatened to blow up the entire station unless we gave in to his demands."

"How did he manage that?" Mickey asked. "I mean, he couldn't have brought a bomb aboard with him in his luggage."

"He had extensive training in demolitions, and he had access to our onboard armory. He had a bandolier of grenades slung across his chest, plus another in his hand. He told us that when his grenade went off, it would trigger a series of explosions that would blow the station to pieces."

"Obviously that didn't work," I said.

Musa shook his head. "I managed to shut off the artificial gravity throughout the station the instant before he blew himself up. As I'd hoped, that wreaked havoc with the switches he'd installed in the other explosives around the station."

"That's why you took so long to bring the gravity back up," Romeo said.

"Our technical teams worked as fast as they could. We've ejected all stray explosives into space rather than attempting to disarm them on a functioning station."

"At least we only lost Captain O'Day," I said as I thought of her scorched body.

Musa frowned. "We very nearly lost Jun as well. He launched himself at our terrorist at the same moment I turned off the gravity. He managed to bat the grenade out of the man's hand. That was the explosion that killed Captain O'Day."

"And what happened to Jun?" I asked. The man had always seemed untouchable.

"The explosion—along with the lack of gravitation reinforcement—compromised the viewport in the rec room. While he was struggling with the terrorist, they smacked into it, and it gave way. I managed to find a handhold and pull myself to safety, but Jun and our traitor were pulled out into space. Jun is currently in our infirmary, recovering from his exposure to raw vacuum."

"How the hell did even he manage that?" Romeo said.

"He wasn't a Spartan-II, obviously, but Threes were built to last," Musa said, not without some small pride in the older Spartan generations.

"But even people like that are only good for a few minutes at best," I said. "How'd we get him back into the station so quick? Wouldn't the decompression have shot him out into space?"

Musa nodded. "Once Jun was clear of the station and the air escaping from it, he planted his feet on the traitor's chest and kicked off as hard as he could. That propelled him back toward the station, and we were able to recover him in time. He'll be on the mend for a while, but he should do so completely."

"And the traitor?" said Mickey, his voice small.

"Jun's kick sent him farther away from the station. He died before we could recover him."

"No," Mickey said. "I meant, who was he?"

Musa grimaced. "I want you all to understand that this entire incident is to be kept under the strictest confidence, only to be revealed to others under my direct orders, no matter their clearance."

"Is that necessary?" I said, sensing Mickey and Romeo's discomfort.

"The rebooted SPARTAN program is at a delicate stage. News of a security lapse like this getting out could compromise our independence, which is exactly what this little bastard would have wanted. For that reason alone, I'm not willing to let that happen."

I looked to the others, and they both nodded at me. "Understood, sir."

He drew a breath to steel himself. "The traitor was Spartan Rudolf Schein."

"I knew it!" Romeo exclaimed, hitting his fist into an open palm.

"You didn't know nothing," Mickey said. The strain from that horrible day had put dark circles under his eyes. He looked like he wanted nothing more than to press the reset button and start over again.

"Course I did," said Romeo. "I never did trust that guy."

"That's why you stopped him from doing all that?" I said. "Cause if you *did* know something about Schein and didn't try to stop him, you were derelict in your duty, and Captain O'Day died because of it."

I liked Romeo some of the time, but he had a horrible habit of talking through the seat of his pants. Most times I ignored it, but if I hadn't called him on it right then and there, I was afraid that Mickey might have tried to silence him permanently.

Romeo flushed at my words, but he didn't snap back at me. He knew I was right, and for once in his ridiculously fortunate life, he shut his damn mouth.

"It *was* Spartan Schein," Commander Musa said. "His mother had been killed by UNSC troops the year before the Covenant War began."

"Because Mama Schein was part of some kind of colonial rebellion?" I asked.

Musa shook his head. "Not officially. She was caught in the crossfire when the UNSC quashed a rebellion on Persia IX. The young Schein didn't seem to bear a grudge about it. He joined the UNSC when he was old enough. He became a decorated veteran of many battles, and he came to us with his superiors' highest recommendations."

"So what the hell happened?" I asked.

"He was loyal when it came to killing the Covenant," Musa

said. "He turned against us, though, when it came to fighting his own kind."

"We still have plenty of Covenant to mix it up with," Mickey said. "Couldn't we have just sent him to fight them instead?"

"We're soldiers," Musa said. "We fight the threats to the UEG, no matter what form they take. We don't shirk our duty just because those threats share DNA close to our own. From what he said in his final rant, Schein had been planning to mass murder this entire class of Spartan-IVs and anyone else he could take with him. He regarded the Spartans as an ONI tool that would be used to cleanse the colonies of troublemakers by any means necessary."

"I guess he didn't get the memo that we're a separate branch now," I said. "Or maybe he just didn't care."

"What about Wakahisa?" Mickey said. "Why kill him?"

"He'd been trying to recruit Spartan Wakahisa to his cause," said Musa. "When Wakahisa said he'd report him instead, Schein killed him."

Mickey let loose a string of curses that would have made my uncle Lou blush. No one saw fit to disagree with him. "And then he tried to frame *me* for it."

Romeo nodded in a rare show of sympathy. "And he did such a feeble job of it. Must have just been trying to buy himself a little time. I mean, I could think of lots of better ways to frame you for something."

I shot him a dirty look. "You two have maybe been working together for too long."

"Losing soldiers to the Front is an increasing problem for the UNSC," Musa said. "We put every candidate through a rigorous screening process to try to ensure that we only recruit the best and most loyal soldiers into the SPARTAN program."

"Maybe if you didn't send us out to shoot other people," Romeo said. "That might be a big start."

If my glare had been fitted with an assault rifle, Romeo would have been KIA on the spot.

"What?" he said at the chilly response Mickey and I gave him. "We were all thinking it."

"You need to stow that talk," I said to him.

"Hey, I don't know about you, but *I* signed on to fight the Covenant," Romeo said.

Musa cleared his throat, and Romeo finally seemed to realize he'd been mouthing off in front of someone other than his buddies.

"The SPARTAN-II program began before anyone in this part of the galaxy had ever heard of the Covenant," Musa said in the kind of clipped tone that brooked no arguments. "We were created to help squash the Insurrection, and the Front carries on those terrorists' work. These so-called rebels don't want *peace* with the rest of humanity. They're demanding *war*. The appearance of the Covenant didn't end that. It only *interrupted* it."

"All I'm saying is that this shouldn't surprise anyone," Romeo said with a soft voice and a reluctant shrug. "Not one damn bit."

Mickey nodded along with Romeo.

Musa gave them both a weary sigh and then spoke in clear, hard terms. "What's left of the Covenant is still a major threat, and it will be for years. Perhaps forever. Like most of us serving, I prefer to focus on such threats. That said, we Spartans do our duty either way. *Understood?*"

I understood one thing for sure: Our continued careers depended on answering that question properly. I wondered what they would do with a decommissioned Spartan. Would they strip the implants out of us or just deactivate as many of them as they could? Either way, how would that leave you in the end?

I also wondered if any of us would be the first to find out.

"Yes, sir," I said.

"Yes, sir," said Mickey.

Romeo chewed on his lower lip and drew out the drama for as long as he could. In the end, his answer was the same as ours. "Yes, sir."

SIXTEEN

So that's how we wound up on Talitsa the following year. By that point, Mickey, Romeo, and I had been full-on operational Spartans for nearly eighteen months. We'd shaken the bugs out of our systems and become a well-oiled, three-soldier fighting machine.

Up until then, Commander Musa had been as good as his word about what kinds of opponents we'd face. We'd been shipped off to distant corners of the galaxy to fight fractured Covenant forces and beat back any kind of opposition as they attempted to reorganize. You'd be surprised how much damage three Spartans can do, especially when you're not having to worry about a Covenant destroyer coming in overhead and glassing the ground you're standing on. The Covenant always had better spacecraft during the war, but we could hold our own against them on the ground. With their alliance shattered, the remaining leaders either in hiding or on the run, and their fleets broken up, let's just say those were a good few years for the UNSC.

The postwar Covenant mostly broke up into its individual species, each of which had to try to forge a new leadership for themselves for the first time in centuries. The Elites started a civil war with each other that had more factions than I care to count. Some of them even allied with us, including one headed by the Arbiter, who'd helped the Master Chief himself put an end to the Covenant

War. Most of the rest of them were too busy fighting him and each other to bother with us, but we found—and took care of—some notable exceptions.

The Jackals broke up into sects that squabbled with each other like starving dogs fighting over a fresh kill. The Brutes? Without the Covenant imposing any kind of structure on them, they mostly fell to chewing each other to pieces again. All we had to do was bust out the popcorn and watch. Sometimes they'd fall in with an Elite faction trying to resuscitate the Covenant under new leadership, but they rarely had the ability to put aside their differences and execute such a plan on their own.

The Grunts mostly wandered around in lost packs, looking for an alpha to lead them. If they weren't such dangerous little buggers who bore so little attachment to their lives, it almost would have been funny.

Some of the Hunters took up with the Arbiter and his Elites. Others stayed loyal to the Sangheili they'd known before. For us, that meant we sometimes had them on our side, but more often we did not.

The Drones mostly dug in and disappeared. We tried to adopt a "don't poke the nest" policy with them when we could. It didn't always work, but we had plenty of battles to fight already without having to go looking for trouble.

As you might imagine, ONI spent a lot of time and effort trying to track down more of the Huragok. The Covenant may have killed the vast majority of them before we could get our hands on them, or maybe they just fled when the time was right. That said, I've been told that the UNSC managed to rescue a few. I've never seen one working in the SPARTAN program, but I wouldn't be surprised to hear they have a few of them helping out somewhere higher in the chain of command.

The new Spartan branch played a huge role keeping the Covenant safely away from human civilization. Working in coordination with the UNSC, we even wound up saving a few aliens sometimes, too. Commander Musa called that a great way to make friends and cement alliances.

Back before I met Vergil, I don't know how excited I would have been about doing something like that. Working with that Huragok, though—and being trapped in that orbital station with him for those few weeks back in 2552—taught me well that not all aliens have it in for humanity. Some of them, like Vergil and the rest of the Huragok, weren't even working with the Covenant of their own free will.

The Arbiter—the Sangheili who wound up in charge of the Elites after the war ended—seems like a good sort, too. I'll admit to having some grudging respect for him and his kind, even the ones that I still end up fighting. They have their own sense of honor, which is a lot more than I can say for the Brutes or Jackals.

Still, it was a lot simpler when any alien that came up into my field of vision was a viable target. Fortunately, Commander Musa doesn't send us out to save those buggers dedicated to killing us. If our actions somehow indirectly wind up keeping a few hostile aliens alive a little bit longer, we can only call that "collateral rescue," as opposed to damage.

Hey, it happens.

Despite Musa stating in no uncertain terms that the Spartans were now a separate branch of the UNSC, we still wound up working with ONI on a regular basis. Spartans may be great at lots of things, but we're a bit too big to make for good spies.

Mjolnir armor isn't built for skulking. Unless you get one of the models with the active camouflage upgrade. But even then, you can't exactly tiptoe around in a suit like that.

Because of my working relationship with ONI—and my personal one with Veronica—Alpha-Nine went on several covert missions that made good use of our skill set. In effect, ONI served as our spotters, and we lined up and took the shots.

I was always wary on ONI missions—especially if Veronica wasn't involved. They liked to dole out information to the Spartans on a need-to-know basis, but that often translated into Spartans getting in deeper-than-predicted trouble because we never had the full picture of what was actually going on.

Sometimes it was far worse than that. ONI isn't known for valuing its assets as much as the assets value themselves. From ONI's point of view, sacrificing a few people to save hundreds or even thousands makes solid mathematical sense. If you're one of those to be sacrificed, however, you might want a heads-up about the magnitude of what you've been asked to do.

Blindness takes all the fun out of being a hero.

I trust Veronica to give me a nudge and a wink so I can at least turn in the direction of incoming fire and meet my fate head-on.

So when she told me that Vergil had gotten in trouble while working on Talitsa in 2555, I knew two things.

First, she was right. Alpha-Nine—or what was left of it, at least—stood the best chance of anyone to recover our Huragok friend and his human handler safe and sound.

Second, we couldn't let the rebels keep hold of him. As long as they had control of Vergil, he'd work away at making their lives easier. That was something the UNSC could not tolerate. If we couldn't recover Vergil, we'd have to kill him.

That only made me that much more determined to bring Quick to Adjust home with us. Back in New Mombasa, we'd gone through far too much to save the big, floating gasbag from the Covenant to ever let him die, much less shoot him ourselves.

That just wasn't going to happen. Or so we hoped.

As I mentioned at the start of all this, the long hike out to the rebels' camp didn't do much to put me, Romeo, and Mickey into a good mood. Even with our enhanced muscles, moving around in Mjolnir armor gets tiring after a while. The suits assist us with their own powered hydraulics, but they're meant more for charging into battle than sightseeing.

It spoils you fast.

Still, Alpha-Nine had slogged through worse, swimming through the snake-infested rivers of Charion VI, sledding across the burning sands of New Caracas, and burrowing through the eternal snowdrifts of Gaenir Beta.

You wouldn't think a hike across a rock-dotted desert like that would set us off against each other. But lately, it got to be that I couldn't stand being around the other two if we weren't on the job. We were all professionals and completed the missions, but once we got home we all went our separate ways.

Romeo spent most of his free time living up to his nickname. The man had been a womanizer before, but becoming a Spartan only made it worse. There were enough ladies out there who wanted to give a surgically enhanced soldier a try to keep him busy every night of the week.

Trouble was that wherever he did this—which was pretty much anywhere we had some time to spare—it pissed off those local guys who thought of the area women as theirs. A lot. And most of them didn't bother to distinguish between Romeo and any other Spartan. As they came to hate him, they learned to do the same with us all.

It got so bad that Commander Musa had to take him aside and dress him down, threatening to confine him to UNSC bases at best. That didn't stop Romeo much, although it slowed him down a hair. After that, at least he was a bit more discreet.

Mickey sometimes played Romeo's wingman, but he couldn't live up to Dutch's work in that role. When it got to be too much, he hunted down old friends, either from the ODST days or even back home on Luna before that. After all the showboating Romeo did, I was happy to see him trying to keep a low profile while roaming off base.

Me, I generally tracked down Veronica, if she could be found. She always helped keep everything in perspective.

Just as often as not, though, she disappeared for weeks or longer on one ONI op or another. That only served to remind me what a rotten married couple we'd be for each other—at least until we decided to one day hang it all up and retire to a long-forgotten beach somewhere.

When I couldn't find her, I generally kept close to the bases and hung out with the Spartan leadership. There aren't any ranks in the Spartans, as Commander Musa likes to remind me about once a week. Still, some of us are more equal than others. I might not have been a gunnery sergeant anymore, for instance, but I'd been leading Mickey and Romeo too long for them to not jump to action when I started barking orders.

So I kept at it. Everyone's got their role, after all, and I knew mine cold.

Every now and then, I'd catch up with Dutch and Gretchen. Leaving combat duty had treated him well. I don't think I'd ever seen him smile so much when he was part of Alpha-Nine.

"How's Romes?" he'd ask me every time though. Seems the two of them didn't chat much anymore.

Back in the day, they'd been joined at their holsters. You never saw one of them without the other. They knew each other's moves so well, they worked together like longtime dance partners.

I think Romeo took it personally when Dutch left. Maybe they had some kind of in-together-out-together pact that was violated. Either way, Dutch had clearly made the right call. All you had to do was watch him put his arm around Gretchen, and you just knew.

And I thought about the Rookie a lot.

I'd lost a number of soldiers under my command over the years. It's part of the job, the nature of war, etc. But it wasn't the Rookie himself so much as the way he went out. All the rest of my siblings in arms were KIA at the hands, guns, grenades, blades, needles, blasts, or claws of the Covenant. I'd never had another human kill one of us before on my watch.

I didn't always feel too human, but I couldn't blame that on the SPARTAN program. That started soon after I joined the UNSC. Combat can do that to you.

Understand that when I felt that gun tap me in the back of my helmet that day on Talitsa, I knew I'd come to a crossroads for that issue. I just didn't know which way I'd wind up going.

And on that note, you should know that we're sort of back to where we started with my story. Here's what happened next.

SEVENTEEN

When I heard Romeo and Mickey warning me not to move as I lay on the top of that ridge overlooking the Front base, I thought they might be playing some kind of joke on me, but it didn't make much sense.

I'd drilled barrel and trigger discipline into their heads for years, and I'd made sure to revisit it when we became Spartans. We'd seen too many people get hurt or killed by goofing around with guns, and none of us tolerated those sloppy kinds of accidents.

It sure felt like a gun barrel on my helmet, but I held out hope that it was something else, like one of my teammates just trying to get my attention. Mjolnir armor is tough enough that a finger on a gauntlet could smack you like a steel rod.

When I tried to get up and got a second knock in the head, I knew something was definitely up.

Both Mickey and Romeo had warned me to stay down, and while I can be a little contrary by nature, I'd already lived a lot longer by trusting and listening to my teammates. I didn't see a good reason to doubt their word here.

"Okay. This is an awful bad time for a joke," I said, still holding out hope for the least painful explanation.

And then the rebels stood up to surround us. They didn't

charge up at us out of the camp, or drop down out of the sky, or appear out of thin air like camouflaged Elites.

Goddammit, they'd been waiting for us.

Lying in wait for as long as it had taken us to hike up to that spot and start spying on them ourselves.

They had not only been told we were coming, but we were led right to where they could get the drop on us.

You might wonder how that could happen if I was in the lead. When you work with teammates for long enough, you develop an unspoken language, a means of communicating by the way your bodies move. All it takes is for one of you to start pushing or lagging in one direction or another to guide the rest of the crew.

Most of the time, it's on instinct, honed over the years, and it keeps getting you out of tough spots in one piece. You don't question it—or your teammates' instincts either.

But it's not so hard for someone on the team to pull the others where you want them to go if you have a destination in mind.

In fact, it's practically invisible. Unless you're actively working against it, you just go with it.

The funny part was that, at first, I couldn't tell who the problem was. Who'd betrayed me? Was it Romeo, Mickey, or—worst of all—both?

"Gunny?" Romeo said. "I don't think anyone's laughing."

Then I figured it out.

Romeo had said, *Hold it right there, Gunny. Don't make one damn move.*

Mickey had said, *Better listen to him, Buck. Don't move a muscle.*

None of us ever called each other by our real names unless we had something serious to discuss—and I mean life-and-death or court-martial-at-least serious. Especially when we didn't have any officers around.

They were both warning me to stay down, but one of them was also warning me about the other.

I twisted my head around slowly to see Romeo had his weapon at the ready. But it was pointed at the rebels rather than me.

Much as Romeo grated on me, he hadn't betrayed me.

That meant it was Mickey.

"Dammit, Spartan Crespo," I said. "You picked one hell of a time to mix up the good guys and bad guys."

Mickey didn't say a word. He just ground the barrel of his gun into the back of my helmet. I could hear the sand under its tip scratching my armor's paint.

That armor was fantastic, but the colors on it never held up. It always came back from every mission scratched, scraped, and dinged to hell. And that was the way we liked it. The UNSC may have given Commander Musa carte blanche to rebuild the SPAR-TAN program, but he'd been wise enough to put those efforts into things like training and performance rather than worrying about cosmetics.

Besides the paint and the laminated layers of deflectives, my armor also came fitted with personal shields, a force field that enveloped me and protected me from incoming munitions. It would take a lot more than a single round from Mickey's gun to kill me.

The trouble was that taking that round would rob my shields of a lot of their power. Even if I'd been able to turn around and start fighting back at Mickey without him getting another shot off first, he'd be able to take down my shields before I could do the same to him. And then my armor, as good as it was, wouldn't keep me alive for much longer.

Sure, Romeo might have been able to help me out. Together, we should have been able to take Mickey down in no time flat. But Mickey wasn't alone.

We had something like forty rebels surrounding us, maybe more. I couldn't tell for sure at the time, with my face half planted in the dirt. They carried an assortment of mix-and-match rifles and wore the kind of battle armor that I'd first been issued when I started with the ODSTs, although they'd painted it a rusty camouflage pattern to help them blend in with the local terrain.

Few of their weapons or suits of armor matched up well. The Front didn't have the robust supply chain of the UNSC, and I suspected they'd mostly stolen their gear from wherever they could find it. Some of them had probably even walked off with it when they'd gone AWOL from the UNSC.

"Good work, Michael," one of the rebels said in a gravelly voice as he lifted the faceplate on his armor. "We'll take it from here." He stood up right in front of me and stalked straight toward us.

I'd seen his type before. He had a graying, well-trimmed mustache and the kind of eyes that came across as painfully sincere no matter what he was jawing about. His armor didn't fit him well, and he swung his gun around on his hip like it was a baby. I figured he shot off his mouth more often than his weapon. He clearly hadn't served in the UNSC, and probably saw that as a badge of honor.

"If you're going to kill me, just do it now and get it over with," I said. "You'll save me the agony of having to listen to your revolutionary bullshit."

The rebel leader chuckled. No one else moved a centimeter. "Now, you don't think you're getting off that easy, do you?" he said. "A live Spartan's a valuable thing."

"You already got Mickey in the bag for you," I said. "Don't see why you need any of the less helpful variety."

"That's not how this is going to go," Mickey said. "Try keeping your mouth shut for once, and we'll all get out of this alive."

"Right," I said, half turning around on my belly. "I can tell how concerned you are about my health by the way you stuck your gun against my head."

About half the rebels in the circle took a step forward and leaned toward me with their weapons. The rest of them kept their guns trained on Romeo, who presented the bigger threat, since he wasn't flat on the ground. I banked on the ones keeping their weapons trained on me not wanting to shoot me and their new pal Mickey over a few words, but I knew there was only so much play in the rope they'd caught me with.

Mickey stuck his knee in my back and forced me flat on my chest again.

"Actually, your chances of living to a ripe, old age just sky-rocketed," the rebel leader said. "As did those of everyone who meets you."

"I don't know," I said. "I just met you, and I'd say your odds just went through the floor."

The man leaned forward and got on one knee right there in front of me. "I've had a lifetime of jingoistic idiots like you pushing me and my people around. You cost me my son. You're goddamn lucky I didn't have you killed on sight."

"If you can't find your balls, maybe you could borrow Mickey's."

That actually got a chuckle out of a few of the other rebels, and their leader's cheeks flushed red. Then he bent over and spit onto my faceplate.

"Don't push him, Dr. Schein," Mickey said to the rebel leader. "Buck may be on the wrong side of this war, but he helped win the last one."

"Schein . . . ?" Romeo's voice went up an octave in surprise. "Oh, you gotta be kidding me."

I was just as shocked. Our rebel captor had the same last name as the Spartan recruit who tried to frame Mickey for murder? It's too big a galaxy for something like that to be a coincidence.

"I met him at Rudolf's funeral," Mickey said.

"Seriously, Mickey? You went to that asshole's funeral?" I shook my head.

"That asshole even had a funeral?" said Romeo.

Dr. Schein kicked me in the face for that one. Didn't hurt me at all, though I couldn't help hoping he broke a toe trying.

"Funerals," the doctor's voice cracked, "are how civilized people say good-bye to the people they care about. The people they respect. The people they love. Decent. People."

"Your *decent* son killed a Spartan who hadn't done a damn thing except sign up at the same time as him," I said. "Not to mention killing a fantastic UNSC captain while trying to take himself out and all of us with him."

The doctor hefted his rifle at me. The thing looked like an antique compared to the gear we were toting around, but it had a barrel I could have jammed my thumb into. The bullet that fit a bore that wide would put one hell of a dent in my shields at this range.

"You're a very persuasive man." Dr. Schein's voice wavered. "I think you've convinced me that you're not worth the trouble of keeping alive."

Mickey spun his rifle about and slammed the butt of it into the back of my head. That cracked the glass in my faceplate, and even with my helmet on, I saw stars. "Shut up, Buck!" he said. "Or someone's going to grant you that death wish of yours."

Romeo started forward then, but he only got a step before Mickey flipped his rifle back over and stuck it in Romeo's face. Every one of the rebels swung their rifles in his direction simultaneously. If I hadn't had Mickey kneeling on my back right then, I might have been able to take advantage of that.

"Back up, Romes," Mickey said. "We'd like you both alive."

"Right," Dr. Schein said in my direction. "But since we have two of you, we could consider the other one a spare."

They weren't fooling me. If they had Mickey on their side, *both* Romeo and I were spares. The mileage they'd get out of two Spartans captives was nothing compared to what a Spartan converted to their cause would mean. While ONI might try to squelch the news, Spartans got killed all the time.

They never switched sides.

I only hoped that if I had to die that day, I'd be able to take Mickey with me. At least I'd rob them of that.

I wanted to spin around and rip his head from his shoulders right then and there. I was so furious I could hardly see straight.

"One little talk with this jackass, and suddenly you've switched sides? What about everything we've done together, Mickey? How many times have I saved your life?"

"How many times have you put it in danger? How many times did you haul us all into a firefight we should have avoided? I didn't get the Rookie killed, Buck. Goddammit, that was *you*!"

"Is that what this is all about? Some sick and twisted version of survivor's guilt stuck in your head because you couldn't pull the trigger when you needed to? You want to ask these guys to give me a minute, I can put an end to that trouble for you!"

"Hell, I'd be happy to hold him down for you, Gunny," Romeo said.

Mickey ignored him and kept his rage focused on me. "So I could be just another notch in your service record? How many troopers died under your command, Buck? Do you even remember all of their names? Serving with you, getting killed is just a matter of time!"

"I did all right by you. Better than you did by the Rookie!"

"We should never have been fighting other humans! Don't you get that?"

I spun around underneath him, and he leaped away before I could grab him. The rebels shoved the barrels of their rifles at me, but I kept screaming at Mickey instead. *Do you mean exactly like you're doing right now?*

Mickey leveled his gun at my chest. "You, Spartan Edward Buck, are under arrest by the United Rebel Front. I hereby declare you our prisoner of war."

I glared at him so hard I wondered if I might melt my armor's faceplate.

"What?" Romeo said. "Don't I get any of that formal combatant love?"

I didn't say a word. I just held my hands over my head while the rebels stripped me of my weaponry. They did the same to Romeo, who whined out loud about every piece they took from him.

"What about their armor?" one of the rebels said.

"It's a couple hundred kilos, and it requires robotic machinery to get in and out of it," Dr. Schein said. "I think we'll let them carry it back to the base for us."

It was only about a klick to the Front base, but it felt like the longest walk of my life. The bowl of the steep-sloped valley had a bit more vegetation scattered about it than the rocky desert we'd marched through to get here, but that only meant a few scrub brushes here and there and a hardy tree or two that was just too scrawny and stubborn to die. Boulders of all sizes lay tumbled between us and the hangar in which I could still see Vergil's blue glow, including a few rock formations I could have hidden a Warthog behind.

I was glad that Vergil was safe, but I hadn't seen Sadie yet. I wondered what they might have done to her. Hopefully her

rapport with the Huragok meant that Sadie was too valuable to the
rebels for them to have gotten rid of her.

Either way, if I wanted to make sure Vergil and hopefully
Sadie didn't get hurt, I didn't have many options. Sure, I could
let Mickey and the rebels do whatever they wanted to me, but I
absolutely hated that idea. I refused to let those jackasses get away
with this, and I'll admit, a large part of me burned to beat the crap
out of Crespo.

My only other choice was to try something before we reached
the hangar. Once we got there, the chances of the Engineer—or
Sadie, if she was there, too—taking a stray round went up expo-
nentially. I just had to find the right moment to make my move
before it became too late.

Dr. Schein led the way down the slope, weaving his way
through the boulders. Romeo and I walked side by side while the
rest of the rebels formed a wide semicircle behind us, all with
their weaponry at the ready and leveled at us. I wondered if the
good doctor would be caught in friendly fire if Romeo and I made
a break toward the man.

Mickey walked right behind Romeo and me, covering us both
with his assault rifle. Alone, even unarmed, Romeo and I might
have been able to take him—at least before he killed us both—but
not with forty armed rebels giving him a hand.

I craned my neck around to look back at him through my
cracked faceplate. "I can't believe you, Mickey, you stinking
bastard. You just betrayed everything you've been fighting for
your entire adult life. Worse than that, you betrayed Romeo
and me!"

"And over the Rookie, too?" Romeo snorted. "Took you a long
time to find the guts to turn on us, didn't it?"

"I wanted to resign after that," Mickey told us. "I even put in my paperwork. Then Jun contacted me to recruit me to become a Spartan."

I sneered at him. "And you saw your chance to become the greatest traitor the UNSC has ever known?"

"I thought you were one of the good guys," Romeo said with a sad shake of his head.

"I was." Mickey hesitated. "I still am."

"When the Covenant War ended, the UNSC didn't fold up shop and send its heroes home," Dr. Schein said. "Like any other war powers throughout history, once they'd dominated the realm they'd fought so hard over, they weren't about to give it up. They took those brave men and women who'd battled so well against humanity's common foe, and they turned them against their fellow humans, who only wanted to be left to themselves."

Romeo started to laugh.

"What's so funny?" Mickey said.

"So much!" Romeo said. "Well, two things, really. And I can't decide which is better!"

He giggled himself silly then, and I couldn't help but join in. We kept walking through it all, waiting for him to catch his breath.

"Maybe you can help me out here, Gunny," Romeo said. "What's funnier? All this bullshit the man here's spouting? Or the fact that Mickey bought it?"

Mickey didn't see any humor in that. "Shut the hell up."

"Oh, wait!" Romeo said, almost crying with laughter. "Maybe it's the fact that Mickey's going to go down in the books as an even bigger traitor than his parents! I mean, after trying to live that down his whole life? And there he goes to follow in their footsteps?"

Mickey stepped forward and smashed his rifle into Romeo's

back. The man went tumbling down the slope toward the camp, head over heels. He crushed a scrub brush as he rolled over it, and he glanced off the side of a boulder, too, but it looked like his shields held, keeping him safe the entire way.

Other than shouting "Whoa!" as he went over, he laughed the whole way down.

For someone of Dr. Schein's education, he displayed a stunning command of profanity as he sent the rest of his soldiers down the hill after Romeo, who kept rolling away.

I turned around and found myself staring down the barrel of Mickey's weapon.

"So tell me, Spartan Crespo," I said as the others chased down Romeo. "Sorry, I mean *Traitor* Crespo. What so disgusted you about your job and your friends that you decided to turn against them?"

"You already know. You've seen the same things as me. You've been sent to kill the same people." I could almost hear him grind his teeth. "You *know*."

"I know how fast those people you're talking about turned against us as soon as the war was over. I don't think our guns had even cooled off after saving their asses from the Covenant."

"And did we ever question our orders to stop shooting aliens and start murdering our own kind?"

I couldn't help but bark a short, bitter laugh. "Any time we weren't actually under fire, you and the rest of Alpha-Nine questioned your orders constantly. You really think I was just some ONI drone relaying instructions to you guys?"

"I signed up to fight the Covenant."

"You signed up. Period. And you could have mustered out at any damn point. You joined the Spartans instead."

"I thought they'd send us out to kill more Covenant."

"We kill bad guys, aliens or not."

"Bad guys?"

Schein turned away from watching the others chase after Romeo. "You're wasting your breath, Michael. From what you've told me about his relationship with Captain Dare, Mr. Buck is too much an ONI man to ever change."

That accusation annoyed me, but it wasn't surprising.

Mickey scoffed at me. "You know, during your Spartan transformation, you spent so much time with Veronica, Romeo and I hardly even saw you. That's when I met Rudolf. That's when he opened my eyes to both the UNSC and you."

That stopped me in my tracks. Mickey hauled up fast and jabbed his rifle at me. "Are you telling me you knew about Schein's bullshit even back then?"

"How do you think he got into my footlocker?" Mickey said. "He used to drop dissolving pamphlets about the Front in there for me to read. Hell, I gave him the code."

"You gotta be goddamn kidding. And then he betrayed you by trying to frame you for Wakahisa's murder? *I stood up for you about that!*"

"He just needed to buy some time to put the rest of his plan in place," Dr. Schein said. "Sadly, it wasn't enough."

"I don't know what kind of crap this guy's been filling your skull with over the past few months, Mickey, but do me one favor based on the years we've worked together—the countless times we've had each other's backs? Don't fling that same shit at me."

Mickey started in on the excuses straightaway. "There comes a time when a man has to—"

Having a gun pointed at my head by someone I'd trusted with my life more times than I could count was one thing. Listening to him spout that kind of revolutionary bullshit at me *really* pissed me off. "Don't you 'In the course of human events' me, Spartan!" I snarled. "This isn't ancient history, and you aren't on the side of angels!"

Mickey grunted at that. "Fine," he said. "Don't listen. Keep your ears closed. Just be a good little soldier and do what you're told."

"Maybe you should have stuck to that plan yourself. I guess I should have seen this coming. Forgive me for thinking you might not wind up like your parents."

"Hey." Mickey's voice went cold.

"How old were you when they died, again? And which government building on Luna were they trying to blow up for the insurrectionists?"

"That's got nothing to do with this. I was too young to even remember much about them. I faithfully served the UNSC for my entire life—"

"Until now. But you had to enlist, didn't you? Mandatory for all foster care kids."

"I put in my two years, and then I re-upped. ODST was my home!"

He started to say something else, but I put up a hand to interrupt him.

"Hey, I know. It's a whole new kind of war these days." I stepped closer to him. "But you had the chance to muster out, and you became a Spartan instead. And then you sold us out. Just like those parents of yours who you say you never knew."

"I'm not like them!" he shouted at me in a thick, hoarse voice.

"I guess you're right." I sneered at him. "They might have been traitors—just like you—but at least they weren't wearing a uniform when they did it."

I tapped Mickey right in the chest as I said that, and that

pushed him straight over the edge. He hauled back on his rifle to take a full swing at me.

If I hadn't gotten him so upset, he probably would have realized what a stupid move that was. When he opened his stance for his swing, I came at him and knocked his weapon away with my left arm. As it arced off into the distance, I punched at him with my right and clocked him in the jaw.

"Michael!" Dr. Schein shouted. "No!"

Mickey was too angry to listen. He dove at me, howling like an animal.

Uphill as he was, this made it easy for him to knock me down the slope, and I wasn't about to fight him on that. Instead, I wrapped my arms around his waist and brought him with me.

We didn't tumble as far down as Romeo, which was perfect. We had just enough distance from Schein that he wouldn't want to shoot for fear of hitting us both, but we stopped well shy of the rebels who were still chasing Romeo down.

Away from any other threats, Mickey and I laid into each other with everything we had. With our enhanced Spartan forms, we landed punches on each other that would have shattered regular soldiers' bones—and we survived them.

Downslope, Romeo saw that I had gotten loose, and he took that as his cue to stop tumbling and start tussling. He rolled to his knees, facing upslope, and ground to a halt, ready to face the forty armed fools coming after him—just like he'd always planned it that way.

He scooped up a fist-sized rock and whipped it at the nearest rebel. It caught the man in his armor's faceplate and shattered it. He flopped over like a rag doll, and his rifle skittered down the slope ahead of him.

Romeo hurled another couple rocks at the rest of the rebels.

He caught one in the leg, shattering her knee, and he knocked the gun out of another one's hands.

The rebels realized that the man they'd been chasing had only been toying with them until now, and they scrambled for cover. If they'd had some discipline—and a decent commander leading them—they might have opened up concentrated fire on Romeo instead and overwhelmed him with their sheer numbers.

Then they might have had a chance.

Romeo leaped forward and snatched up the fallen rifle next to him. He quickly checked its action, saw it was good, and then started picking off the rebels one by one.

Meanwhile, Mickey was doing his level best to beat the tar out of me.

I don't know if I've ever heard of two fully armored Spartans going at each other with everything they had. Sometimes we'd spar with each other for training purposes, but that was in a dojo or a ring and dressed in shorts and shirts.

We held back during sparring—just a little, at least. As well-trained and hyper-boosted combat machines, we knew all too well how easy it was for us to kill someone, and we didn't want any accidents during training. We always had a medic on hand, just in case.

This was nothing like that. The exact opposite, in fact.

Mickey didn't give me any space. To be fair, neither did I.

We pounded the hell out of each other.

Romeo later told me that it sounded like thunder rolling down the slope. If that's so, both of us kept bringing the lightning.

Mickey had been a brawler back in school, mostly fighting people who gave him a hard time about his parents. After he enlisted, the UNSC had trained him to be a far better fighter than that, with much better weaponry, and I'd watched him develop into one hell of a trooper.

In a fistfight, though—struggling for his life with someone he'd considered a friend for years—he fell back on those old-school habits. They mostly involved hitting as hard and fast as he could, hoping to knock the wind out of me or just scare me enough that I backed off.

I'd seen Mickey spar, and he made the same mistakes in the ring, too, no matter how many times I'd try to coach him out of it. He came at me hard and fast, and I saw I could finally teach him the lesson he'd been begging for. I did what he least expected: I covered up, braced myself, and let him hit me.

When his first punch landed, I thought maybe I'd made a mistake. My right to his jaw had loosened what little grip he had on his temper, and he fueled his biceps with that rage.

He aimed for my cracked faceplate and hit me with a sledgehammer cross that I caught on my shoulder instead. I let it knock me backward, but kept my footing.

He came at me again and again and again, trying to slug me in the faceplate, each blow like a shotgun blast at point-blank range, but I kept blocking him with my shoulder.

My shields did their best to protect me, but they could only handle so much. When they finally gave out, I felt the plating there start to crack, and I realized that he wasn't going to tire himself out before he pounded his way straight through my armor.

When he threw his next blow, I leaned to the left and dodged, and he overbalanced himself. I grabbed him by his right shoulder and hauled him over my leg, throwing him face-first into the ground.

He skidded down the slope, trying to find purchase with the heels of his hands. I dove after him and landed on his back. Then I grabbed the back of his helmet and began to slam his faceplate into the rock-strewn dirt until it cracked open like a rotten egg.

It took forever, but my own anger lent me strength. Eventually his shields gave, and the faceplate—which was weaker than the armor on my shoulder—shattered.

Mickey managed to get one arm under himself and shoved upward hard enough to spin around onto his back. I stayed on top of him, straddling him, slamming him with my fists.

I kept hammering at his faceplate. I could see his eye staring at me through the hole I'd made in its silvered surface, wide with fury and terror.

I cocked back my right fist for a devastating blow, but as it came down, he grabbed my forearm and stopped it. I tried the same with my left, and he blocked me the same way.

"Gunny!" he said. "Wait!"

I don't think he really expected me to—and I didn't.

I couldn't.

He'd already spoiled every bit of trust he'd ever earned from me. He'd thrown it all away to join up with the Front. He'd spat not only on the ODST and the SPARTAN program, but on our friendship.

On our brotherhood.

This was the only shot Romeo and I had for getting out of this alive—much less completing our mission—and I wasn't about to throw it away by hesitating to take down another human being. Not even a former pal.

Not the way he'd let the Rookie die.

While Mickey held my wrists, I spread my arms apart and dove forward, smashing the forehead of my helmet into his faceplate, shattering it.

I didn't feel his nose give way—my helmet protected me from that—but his arms went limp. When I drew back, I saw blood streaming out of his face, the fight gone out of him.

I looked down at him for a moment. I wasn't sure if he was shamming or maybe I'd killed him. With the adrenaline pumping through me, though, I was ready to go at him again if he made another wrong move.

That's when Dr. Schein shot me in the back.

My armor slowed down the bullet, but the impact knocked me down the slope. It hurt like hell, as if someone had shoved a red-hot hook right through my lower back.

If I hadn't been in the middle of a fistfight with Mickey, my armor's shielding might have deflected the shot. As it was, I had nothing but the armor plating itself between me and the bullet, and that proved not to be enough.

Fortunately, my armor hadn't stopped working. It automatically sealed the hole the bullet had made, keeping me from bleeding out, and injected me with a flood of biofoam, which brought the agony down from blinding to almost tolerable.

By the time I could breathe again, I flopped over on my back and found Schein stalking toward me down the slope, his rifle aimed at my head. I glanced farther downslope and saw Romeo having his way with the rest of the rebels. They'd scattered before him like rats trying to escape a hungry lion. The only chance they had was to run, but he was so much faster. It was no contest.

Still, they'd keep him too busy to help me until it was far too late.

"You sons of bitches!" Schein said as he drew closer. "We tried to do this as peaceably as possible, but you couldn't help but ruin it. We didn't even get you into the camp!"

"Best laid plans," I said with a groan. "I didn't think one of my own teammates would betray me today either."

"Just stay right where you are!" he said. "Don't you dare try anything else!"

This guy had me dead to rights, and I didn't doubt he'd kill me once he realized that Romeo was destroying the rest of his squad. In a one-on-one fight against any Spartan alive, none of them would walk away.

Given my state then, I might have been the one exception to that rule.

He came to a halt about five meters away. He'd seen what I'd done to Mickey, and he wasn't about to give me an opportunity to do the same to him. "I'm telling you, do not move!"

I froze, but I kept glancing around in my helmet. If I could have found a rock nearby, I'd have chucked it at Schein like Romeo had at his own attackers.

Just my luck that I had to land in the one spot on the entire damn slope that didn't have any at hand.

"I should just shoot you right now," Schein said.

"Can I at least take off my helmet?" I said, wheezing as hard as I could.

"What?" He'd heard my words, but they didn't make any sense to him.

"Lungs filling up. Can't breathe," I said, hacking.

He frowned as he considered it. I don't think he knew for sure at that point if he wanted me alive or dead.

Maybe the fact he was a doctor—someone supposedly dedicated to saving lives rather than taking them—helped him make up his mind.

"Fine," he said with a nod. "Do it. But don't try anything funny."

He didn't lower his gun. I fumbled with the catch on my helmet. I failed.

"Hurry up!" He glanced down the slope at Romeo tearing through his troops. The entire plan had apparently hung on

Mickey's betrayal, and with him down, Schein could see it all falling apart.

I gave my helmet another shot, and this time it came free. I pulled it off and barely caught it with one hand before it went tumbling down in Romeo's direction.

I gasped for air, but it didn't help me much. The problem wasn't really with the helmet anyhow, but with the man pointing a gun at me.

More gunshots rang out below, and Schein scowled in their direction. He couldn't decide if he should shoot me in the head and then go down to help out his troops or not. He grimaced and stabbed the barrel of his rifle at me and then took a step toward me.

"Get up," he said. "I'm not done with you yet."

I shoved myself up into a sitting position like an old man on a ventilator.

"Spartan Agu!" Schein called down the slope. "I have your sergeant! Lay down that gun, or I'll shoot him in the head!"

"So that's how it is," I said. "Back to the same old threats?"

He ignored me. "Spartan Agu!"

Romeo stood up from behind a boulder downslope. "What? Can't you see I'm busy with these idiots?"

"You bastard!" Schein gaped at Romeo's brazen violence.

I'd been holding my helmet behind me by the edge near the chin. When the barrel of Schein's gun wavered from me, I brought my arm around in a sweeping arc and hurled that tin can at him like it was a harpoon.

It caught him right in the chest and knocked him over on his back. I ignored the pain lancing through my side with every movement and flung myself at him.

He brought his rifle up to blast me away, but I was already

inside the barrel's reach. All he could do was smash the side of it against me.

I sat on his chest and snatched the weapon away from him. It was too long for me to turn it on him, so I used the shoulder stock to pound him in the face instead.

His cheap, stolen armor had nothing on Mickey's or mine. I cracked his helmet in half with a single blow, and the force of it knocked him cold.

I slowly stood and surveyed the situation. Mickey and Dr. Schein were down, and armored rebel bodies littered the slope below me. Down in the bottom of the valley, I saw additional personnel scrambling around, looking for a way to escape—and probably to take Vergil with them.

Romeo waved at me. I put on my helmet, and I could hear him over the comm again.

"You all right?"

"Schein just got it worse," I said, "but I'm not good. Took a high-caliber round in my left side."

"You can still walk?"

"Hell, I can still fight. Just maybe not for too long. Let's go get Vergil before these clowns figure out a way to fly off with him."

"What about Mickey?"

He had a point. I hadn't killed Mickey, but maybe leaving him alive up there on the slope while we went down to rescue the Huragok wasn't such a good idea. My suit had kept me going, and I knew his would be working overtime to get him up and about as soon as it could, too.

I frowned and then nodded down at the rebel camp. "You think you can handle them on your own?"

"Be simpler to put a bullet in his head."

"Just answer the question."

Romeo nodded. "I think they put about everything they had into catching us."

I started trudging back up the slope. "That turns out to not be true, you give me a shout."

"I'm on it," he said as he charged off in the other direction.

I collected Schein's rifle as I worked my way up toward Mickey. He was still out when I got there.

I checked him for any holdout weapons and removed a combat knife and a pistol from his armor. I doubted he had any other ordnance on him—but then I'd figured him to be a good teammate up until that point, too, so I checked him over a second time.

I found another knife, a little T-handled thing meant to be held in your fist as you punched your foe. The kind you used to stab someone in the back.

I threw the damn thing as far as I could.

Then I trudged a bit farther up the slope, sat down on the most comfortable rock I could find, and laid Schein's gun across my lap. From there, I watched Romeo tear through the camp, hunting for trouble.

Every now and then, I'd glance down at Mickey and have to restrain myself from pointing the rifle in his direction and perforating him. I didn't know how I was going to explain this to Commander Musa or Jun. Or even Veronica.

Goddammit. I'd known Mickey for years. We'd helped save *humanity* together. I thought I could have relied on him for anything. How could he *do* this?

Yet maybe that's what blinded me to his treachery. I hadn't entertained even the possibility that he might go rogue like that and betray us all. It still seemed inconceivable.

Maybe that's why I didn't kill him. I wanted to see him go through a court-martial. I wanted to see him try to explain himself. I wanted to watch him as the prosecutor tore through his lies.

And I wanted him to suffer for it for a long, goddamn time.

"You're looking good from up here," I told Romeo over the comm in my armor's collar. I spotted a small squad of five rebels heading his way. "You got a few wannabe heroes coming your way on your ten o'clock."

He didn't reply. He just did his job. Much as Romeo pissed me off sometimes, when it came to getting the work done, there weren't many better.

The rebels weren't outfitted even as well as the ones Romeo had torn through up here on the slope. They wore generic black armor that looked more like it belonged on a police officer than a soldier. It didn't stand up well to Romeo's bullets.

Their return fire never even got past his shields.

From there, Romeo moved into a one-story building that looked like a barracks. I didn't see anyone else enter or leave the place. The walls and ceiling muffled the sound of gunfire from within, but I spotted plenty of muzzle flashes inside, flickering against the windows like strobe lights.

No one else rushed the place. I didn't see anyone running for cover or heading toward a transport to get the hell out of there, which would have been the smart thing to do.

I suppose I shouldn't have expected to see those kinds of smarts in the rebels though.

When Romeo finished in the barracks, he emerged from the other side. From there, he moved into the hangar where I'd spotted Vergil, and I heard a whoop of triumph over the comm.

"Our old gasbag's here, Gunny, and he's got company."

"The welcome kind?" I hadn't heard any shooting inside there yet.

"She says her name's Sadie Endesha."

As down as I was about Mickey, I couldn't help but smile at that.

"Give her a great big Spartan welcome from me."

"Will do," he said, laughing like a schoolboy.

"I don't see a whole lot of other activity down there at the moment," I said. "Wrap up that reunion fast, and make sure our friends are secure."

"Already on it."

I heard a groan from Mickey's direction, just downslope from me.

"Then clear the rest of the buildings and call for a ride home. I got something to take care of up here."

"Roger that."

I waited for Mickey to sit up, facing away from me. He stared down at the bodies scattered along the slope below him and then focused his gaze on the base beyond. "Shit."

For a long moment, I thought he'd gotten stuck on gaping at how sideways his plans for the day had gone. Then I spotted his shoulders shaking. You need to sob pretty hard for that to show through a Mjolnir suit.

I cleared my throat.

Mickey jumped like I'd jabbed him in the spine. He spun around onto his hands and knees and goggled up at me with red, puffy eyes. His tears had washed tracks through the blood on his face.

"Just shoot me, Gunny," he said quietly. "Please."

I can't tell you how much that tempted me. "I've given that a lot of thought while I've been sitting here. More than I probably should have."

I pointed Schein's rifle at him. He gazed right into its monstrous barrel and held his breath.

When I didn't pull the trigger and put him out of his misery, he turned his attention back to me. "So what are you waiting for?"

"I'm not going to do it," I said. "I can't just execute you. We've been through far too much together."

"And I sold you out."

The way he said it sent a chill straight through me. This wasn't something he'd done in the heat of a moment. He'd decided to betray his government, the Spartans, and his teammates, and then he'd set out to do so with all due deliberation.

"That you did, and you're going to have to face justice for it."

"And you think I'm going to survive that?"

"That's not up to me."

He blinked the tears out of his eyes. "You think you're showing me mercy, but you're not. It's the opposite of that."

I glared down at him. "I'm good with that either way."

If he really wanted me to shoot him, all he had to do was attack me again. My sympathy for him would only go so far.

I could see him mulling it over. In the end, though, he was too broken up inside to give it a go. It had taken him everything he had to betray us, and when it all went wrong, he had nothing left.

Instead of rising up at me, he sat back down.

We were still like that when the transport came scudding in over the ridge to collect us.

EIGHTEEN

*Y*ou *did the right thing*, Veronica told me when I finally got ahold of her by viewscreen. I let her say it to me over and over, and I kept hoping that eventually I'd believe it.

To this day, I still don't know. There are so many times when I wish I could go back and put a bullet between Mickey's ears. Or beat his skull to a pulp. Or strangle him until I saw the light go out of his eyes.

And yet I'm grateful that Mickey didn't force my hand.

I've killed lots of people—Covenant and humans alike—but always as part of my job. Mickey's the first person I ever *wanted* to kill with every goddamn fiber, right down to my Mjolnir-clad toes.

Not to stop him from hurting someone, or to keep him from sounding an alarm, or to further any plan or cause.

I mean, I've killed people those ways as part of my job. To defend humanity and serve the greater good.

But I wanted to end him so bad I could taste it. It would have been so simple then, and it would have been over, right?

Ah, bullshit. Even I don't believe that.

Either way, dead or alive, that bastard haunts me to this day.

Vergil and Sadie headed back to Mars with us on our transport. The days of letting the Huragok work in the field—even with a handler like Sadie and a supposedly vetted security detail—were over, and I don't think they minded it. I hear ONI's going to keep them on a much tighter leash after this.

Sadie gave me a huge hug once we were all on the transport together and rocketing for the stars. "I know we've never met," she said, hoisting the tablet she used to communicate with the Engineer, "but Vergil's told me so much about Alpha-Nine over the years, and everything you did for him."

I couldn't help but smile at the Huragok. He leaned into me, and I patted him on his flank. "You know how these guys are," I said with a wistful smile. "They don't know how to lie."

The support crew in the transport stripped Mickey out of his armor as we left Talitsa behind. We shackled his wrists together as well and tossed him in the brig until we got back to base.

I'd never seen another trooper in the brig before, much less a Spartan.

Much less someone I'd considered a brother.

Romeo just shook his head and watched over Mickey the entire trip from a seat in the main cabin. I sat on the far side of the room, with my back to them both. I wanted to be there in case Romeo decided that he'd administer a little justice to Mickey himself, but I feared if I kept watch over Mickey, too, I might succumb to the same temptation.

Mickey didn't say a word the entire time. For a guy who'd spouted a lot of shit when he had a gun on us, he kept awfully silent. I don't think he could bear to confront us or even ponder what his future looked like.

In his head, I don't think he saw one at all.

ONI had a team ready and waiting for us when we landed at the Spartan base on Mars.

"We'll take over from here," the lead agent told me, but I wasn't having any of it.

"No. This one's our responsibility," I said, nodding toward Mickey. "I'm not turning him over to anyone but Commander Musa."

"He betrayed the UNSC," the agent said. "He needs to be tried for high treason."

"He may be a traitor—"

"I think we're pretty clear on that count, Gunny," Romeo said.

I shot a sidelong glare at him and continued. "But he's *our* traitor. Once a Spartan?"

"Always a Spartan." Romeo nodded and then gave the ONI crew a winning smile, paying special attention to the woman in charge. "Right?"

The agent disapproved of our decision—and of Romeo's leer. "With all due respect, a problem like this is an ONI matter."

I stared down at her and her team. "We're Spartans. We don't take orders from ONI. Unless Commander Musa himself calls me up to disagree with me, we're not turning this prisoner over to anyone but him."

ONI agents don't intimidate easily, but I'd just had the worst day of my life since the Covenant glassed Draco III. She saw that in my eyes, did the calculus, and gave way.

She nodded and motioned for her team to step aside. "I'll leave it to people above my pay grade to sort that out."

Romeo and I actually handed Mickey over to Jun. I hadn't seen the man look so grim since the younger Schein had sent him to the infirmary.

I looked at Romeo and gave him a brotherly hug; then we silently walked off to our respective quarters.

That night, after I'd gotten out of my armor and washed the day off me, I got a private video call from Commander Musa over a secure channel. I thought about dodging it for a while—maybe at least until I'd gotten a good night's sleep—but I didn't see the point. We had to have a conversation eventually, and that might as well be now.

I took it in my quarters.

"Good work out there today, Spartan Buck."

"You call all your Spartans to congratulate them after every mission?"

"This was a particularly special mission. In many ways. If we'd have lost the Engineer, that could have been disastrous."

"It wasn't far shy of that anyhow."

"Yes." He steepled his fingers before his face, and his lips drew into a straight, grim line. "Spartan Crespo."

"I'd like to formally apologize for Spartan Crespo's actions, sir, and to submit myself for discipline."

Musa wrinkled his brow at me. "Whatever for?"

"I not only vouched for his character but made his acceptance into the SPARTAN-IV program a condition of my own."

"And you think that makes you responsible for his actions?"

"Doesn't it?"

"Perhaps you think a little too highly of the power of your recommendation." Musa brought down his fingers and allowed himself a gentle smile. "Spartan Jun and I vetted each one of our candidates. If we hadn't thought that Mr. Crespo would make an outstanding addition, we wouldn't have admitted him to the program."

"But one element of that vetting came from interviewing me, and I let you down."

Musa nodded. "Spartan Crespo let us *all* down. We put our trust in others, and sometimes they disappoint us in the worst possible ways. Does that mean we should lash out and look for people onto whom we can shuffle the blame?"

"That's not what I meant—"

He raised a hand to interrupt me. "I know, but if you want to start looking at it that way, then Jun and I are just as responsible for Spartan Crespo's actions as anyone. To some extent, that's true, and we're going to review our procedures and see where and how we went wrong."

"And what do you suspect you'll find?"

Musa shrugged. "Nothing? I'm not sure. Honestly, if I knew, believe me, I would have put a stop to it before we got to this point. But can I tell you something in confidence, Spartan Buck?"

"As long as it's within my security clearance, sir."

He chuckled. "Despite what we tell everyone—despite what the UNSC wants the entire galaxy to believe—Spartans are as human as anyone."

"I'm all too aware of that, sir."

"Good. Just making sure you haven't bought into your own PR. As humans, our new Spartans are liable to make mistakes, and putting our trust in the wrong people sometimes is just as likely as with any of them."

"Your point, sir?"

He paused for a moment to consider his next words.

"When I was to become a Spartan, Dr. Catherine Halsey had me and my fellow teammates abducted at the age of six. Do you know why she did that?"

"The earlier she got her hands on you, the easier it was to make the transformation." Even as I said the words, I could see from his wry eyes that I'd gotten it wrong in exactly the way he'd expected—despite the fact he'd just confirmed all the long-standing rumors about how Spartan-IIs had been recruited by kidnapping.

He gestured toward his wheelchair. "I think you can see by what happened to me that your theory isn't all that true."

"So fill me in. Sir."

"Children are easier to mold. Take them from their homes at such a young age, place them into a barracks, give them the kind of training that teaches them to follow orders, to kill without question, and then you get soldiers you can make real weapons out of. Ones you can always trust."

"You point them at the problem and pull their trigger," I said.

"Exactly. But I firmly believe that ONI got it wrong with the earlier SPARTAN programs. They set out to create infallible weapons. I wanted to take people and forge them into heroes. Very human heroes."

"If you wanted us to be fallible, sir, I have to say you exceeded far beyond my own expectations."

"Fair enough. I understand your disappointment in Spartan Crespo. Hell, I share it, and I'll be answering for it for months. But I still consider the SPARTAN-IV program to be an amazing triumph. And it's not because of Crespo's actions, but yours."

I stared at him, confused, wondering if he was kidding around—or if he'd betray my trust in him instead. "I'm afraid I don't follow, sir."

"How many of the earlier Spartans do you think would have spared Crespo's life? How many of them would have simply put a bullet through his brain instead?"

I shook my head. "That's not something I care to think much about, sir."

"You may not—and I understand that—but I've been contemplating it a lot. Maybe even the Master Chief?"

"Not Jun?"

Musa grunted. "He'd have killed Crespo for sure. But *you* let him live. Because you're not only a Spartan, you're the best kind. The kind with the potential to save us all."

He leaned toward the viewscreen, filling it. "You may be a Spartan, but you're goddamn human, too, and that's something you should be proud of. I certainly am."

"Understood, sir." I struggled for the right thing to say. "I think. Either way, there's just me and Romeo left from Alpha-Nine. That's not much of a fireteam."

"We'll get you reassigned straightaway. No worries on that front. You're too valuable to leave in limbo."

I nodded. "If it's all the same to you, sir, I think I'd like to be *part* of a team rather than leading it. At least for a while."

"Fair enough," Musa said. "Just don't get any ideas about that being permanent."

I gave him a game smile. "I go where I'm needed, sir."

"That's exactly what I want to hear, Spartan Buck," he said. "Dismissed."

I contacted Veronica right after that. I hadn't heard her voice for too long.

We didn't talk about any of this for a good while. Not one word.

Not until now, anyway.

Bam, said the lady.

CODA

"You're breaking up the band?"

Veronica was looking at me in disbelief when I told her I'd finally been assigned to a new fireteam . . . which meant that Alpha-Nine was no more.

"There's not much of a band left. Think of it more like 'me not having to work with Romeo anymore' instead." I couldn't stop the smile that spread across my face as I said that.

She rolled her eyes at me. "That might seem like a huge upside, I'm sure, but at least you *know* Romeo."

"Maybe more than I'd like." I grimaced. "Still, working with someone for years didn't help me out too much with Mickey."

Knowing how upset I could still get about that even three years later, Veronica grabbed the conversation's wheel and yanked it back onto the road. "What do you know about this new team?"

I shook my head. "Not much. Well, not that I can tell you, at least. It's all very hush-hush."

"Can't you even tell me the code name?" She had the kind of twinkle in her eye that you'd see in a kid who'd gotten away with all the cookies in the jar.

"Dammit! You already know, don't you?"

She gave me a mocking shrug. "Little ol' me? Why, how would

one of ONI's top agents know anything about what the most important man in her life is up to?"

She started to walk away from me, but I grabbed her by the hand and pulled her into my arms. Gently, of course. She leaned back and looked up at me, and I just about fell into those deep blue eyes of hers.

"So, I'm important?" I said.

She gave me a quick kiss and then pushed away. "To me, sure. But in the galactic sense?"

"No, *to you* is all I care about," I said.

She turned serious then, the humor fading from her face. "You'll be doing important work. Jameson Locke's one of the best ONI agents around."

"So he keeps telling me."

"That doesn't sound like Locke."

I arched a suspicious eyebrow at her. "So you know what he sounds like?"

She gave me a playful smack across the chest. "Despite what ONI would like you to believe, it's not that big of an organization."

"Especially at the top."

"Exactly."

"Which is why Locke gave me clearance to talk with you about this."

That took her aback. "Really?"

"He figured you'd already know anyhow."

"You mean about Fireteam Osiris?" She paused for me to give her a helpless nod. "He figured right. And Olympia Vale and Holly Tanaka are the best at what they do. Did Locke also tell you what your next assignment is?"

"Yeah, telling you about all this."

She smacked me again, less playfully this time. I flinched like it hurt a lot more than it did. "Your next op."

That got me serious as well. "No. Nothing. I just figured it was your standard go-save-the-galaxy stuff. That's what Spartans do, right?"

"Well, *some* Spartans, anyway."

"We can't all be the Master Chief—wherever the hell he's run off to these days."

Veronica peered up at me, curious. "Was that a hint of admiration in your voice?"

I shrugged. "He's as close to a superhero as humanity has to offer. He's a living legend."

"Didn't think you liked him much."

"Yeah, as an ODST, sure. I thought he was just another bullet-catching glory hound. But once you're inside? And you learn about all the things he did? How many times he saved us all? It's hard to hate on that."

"And how many times he almost got killed. Don't forget that. Superheroes or not, Spartans don't exactly have great life expectancies."

I spread my arms out wide to her. "You're looking at the latest model. New *and* improved."

She stared at me. "Just promise me you'll come back from this one alive."

"I've fought all kinds of things," I said, turning away, "been in all sorts of battles. You never asked me to promise you that before."

"To be honest, I never worried about it all that much."

"It's not like I'm invincible. Contrary to what the press tells you, Spartans *do* die."

Veronica frowned. "I know that. I know what it's like to be in battle, the risks you take as a soldier. Hell, I've been right there alongside you."

"But . . . ?"

"You think it's a coincidence Agent Locke's in charge? He's ONI to the bone."

I put a hand on her shoulder. "That's never put me off before."

"The Spartan branch plans to put Fireteam Osiris up against the worst threats the galaxy has to offer: Covenant remnants, the new rebel insurgency—even some things they're keeping me in the dark on. Heavily classified operations under the worst conditions and with the highest stakes. That's why they have Locke in charge."

I cocked my head at her. "You don't say."

She punched me in the shoulder, hard. If I hadn't seen it coming and rolled with it, she might have broken her knuckles on me.

"Ow!" I rubbed my bruised muscle. "Hey, what the hell was that for?"

"For being so goddamned cocky!" she said. "It's going to get you killed, Buck!"

I reached out and took her in my arms. "Hey," I said as softly as I could manage. "I—I don't mean—it's not like that."

I held her close, and she melted into me. "I'm scared, too," I said. "I don't know what the future holds—for either one of us."

"I'm telling you, these are dangerous days," she said. "Maybe the worst ever."

"For both of us." I brushed her hair out of her eyes and leaned down to kiss her. "Veronica . . . I can't promise you I'll come back alive. You'd know it was a lie."

"A lie I wouldn't mind hearing."

"Fine. But I do promise you this. When I'm on the job with Fireteam Osiris, I'll take it as seriously as a bullet to the heart."

She laid her head against my chest. "Well . . . I suppose that's all I can really ask."

With that, Veronica tilted her head back, gazed into my eyes, and smiled at me as she said the one word I most wanted to hear.

"Bam."

I knew then, that whatever happened—live or die—we'd be all right.

ACKNOWLEDGMENTS

MATT FORBECK

Like any great effort, no book comes together without the help of an amazing team of people. I owe a great deal of thanks to my editor, Ed Schlesinger, who was writing to contact me about this book at the same moment I contacted him. If there are mistakes or troubles in this book, they're mine, and they don't include the many jagged bits that Ed spotted and helped me file smooth.

I also need to thank the fantastic people at 343 Industries—especially Jeremy Patenaude and Tiffany O'Brien, as well as the rest of the writing team—who offered comments and constructive criticism. They were an absolute joy to work with, and the passion and caring they showed for the *Halo* universe spurred me to do my best every step of the way.

On top of that, I'd like to thank all the creators at Bungie, as well, for building such an amazing galaxy for me to play in. That includes Bob Settles, who showed me a demo of what would become *Halo: Combat Evolved* back in 2000, when Bungie was still an independent developer in Chicago. It also includes fellow tabletop game writers like Eric Trautmann and my pal Brannon Boren, who helped write the original *Halo* bible.

ACKNOWLEDGMENTS

343 INDUSTRIES

343 Industries would like to thank Kendall Boyd, Scott Dell'Osso, Matt Forbeck, Isaac Hannaford, Bonnie Ross-Ziegler, Ed Schlesinger, Rob Semsey, Matt Skelton, Phil Spencer, and Carla Woo.

None of this would be possible without the amazing efforts of the Halo Fanchise Team, the Halo Consumer Products Team, Tiffany O'Brien, Kenneth Peters, and Sparth, with special thanks to Jeremy Patenaude.

ABOUT THE AUTHOR

Matt Forbeck is an award-winning and *New York Times* bestselling author and game designer. He has twenty-seven novels and countless games published to date. His latest work includes *Magic: The Gathering* comics, the 2014 edition of *The Marvel Encyclopedia*, his *Monster Academy* YA fantasy novels, and the upcoming *Shotguns & Sorcery* role-playing game based on his novels. He lives in Beloit, Wisconsin, with his wife and five children, including a set of quadruplets. For more about him and his work, visit www.forbeck .com.